BETSY AND TACY GO DOWNTOWN

By the Author

Betsy-Tacy
Betsy-Tacy and Tib
Betsy and Tacy Go Over the Big Hill
Betsy and Tacy Go Downtown
Heaven to Betsy
Betsy in Spite of Herself
Betsy Was a Junior
Betsy and Joe
Carney's House Party
Emily of Deep Valley
The Tune Is in the Tree
The Trees Kneel at Christmas
Betsy and the Great World
Winona's Pony Cart
Betsy's Wedding
The Golden Wedge
(*with Delos Lovelace*)

Adult Fiction by the Author

The Black Angels
Early Candlelight
Petticoat Court
The Charming Sally
One Stayed at Welcome
(*with Delos Lovelace*)
Gentlemen from England
(*with Delos Lovelace*)

BETSY *and* TACY
GO DOWNTOWN

Maud Hart Lovelace

Illustrated

by

Lois Lenski

HarperCollins*Publishers*

First published by Thomas Y. Crowell Company in 1943.
Library of Congress Catalog Card Number 43-51264
ISBN 0-690-13450-9 (lib. bdg.)
ISBN 0-06-440098-0 (pbk.)

FOR HELEN

*and the other inheritors
of Hill Street*

CONTENTS

"I stepped from plank to plank
 So slow and cautiously;
 The stars about my head I felt
 About my feet the sea."

—THE POEMS OF EMILY DICKINSON

THE MAPLE TREE

BETSY was sitting in the back-yard maple, high among spreading branches that were clothed in rich green except at their tips where they wore the first gold of September. Three branches forked to make a seat, one of them even providing a prop for her back. To her right, within easy reach, was another smaller crotch into which a cigar box had been nailed. This was closed and showed on the cover a plump coquettish lady wearing a Spanish shawl.

From this lofty retreat Betsy had a splendid view. It did not look toward the Big Hill where she and her friends Tacy and Tib had had so many adventurous picnics. It looked toward the town. Strictly speaking, her leaf-framed vista was of rooftops going down Hill Street like steps. But Betsy knew whither those steps led.

Sitting in her maple, she was aware of the town, spread out below, of Front Street where the stores were, of streets lined with the houses of people she did not know, of the Opera House, the Melborn Hotel, the skeleton of the new Carnegie Library, and the High School that her sister Julia and Tacy's sister Katie now attended. She was aware of the river winding through its spacious valley and of a world, yet unexplored, lying beyond.

Lifting the lid of the cigar box, Betsy took out a small tablet. It said on the cover, "Ray's Shoe Store. Wear Queen Quality Shoes." She took out a pencil, short and well toothmarked, and chewed it thoughtfully. Then opening the tablet she wrote:

The Repentance of Lady Clinton
by Betsy Warrington Ray
Author of *Her Secret Marriage, The Mystery of the Butternut Tree, A Tress of Golden Hair, Hardly More than a Child*. Etc. Etc.
Chapter One
Lord Patterson's Ball

She had progressed no further when a scratching sound caused her to look down. A red ringleted head was rising toward her. The visitor was Tacy who lived across the street and had been her dear friend for many years. Seven, to be exact, for Betsy and Tacy had started to be friends at Betsy's fifth birthday party, and now they were both twelve.

Tacy paused on a limb just below.

"Is it all right for me to come up?" she asked.

The perch in the maple tree was Betsy's private office. Here she thought out stories and poems and wrote them down. Here she kept what she had written in the cigar box that her mother had given her and Tacy had helped her nail to its present place.

"Of course," said Betsy. "Why weren't you in school this afternoon? Why couldn't you come out to play?"

"Something awful, something terrible has happened," Tacy said. She hoisted herself into a crotch near the one in which Betsy was sitting.

Tacy's large blue eyes swam with tears. Her lids were red, her freckled cheeks were wet. Betsy put her tablet and pencil into the cigar box and closed the lid with the Spanish lady on it.

"What's the matter?" she asked.

Tacy wiped her eyes on a wet ball of handkerchief.

"You remember," she said, "Rena loaned me *Lady Audley's Secret*."

Betsy nodded.

"Well . . . papa found it."

"What happened?"

Tacy's eyes overflowed.

"I had hidden it under the bed. And this noon while we were eating dinner, mamma told papa she thought there was a mousehole in our room, and papa went looking for it, and he found the book.

"He was furious, but he never dreamed it was mine. He marched down to the table and asked Mary whether she'd been reading it, and she said 'no.' And he asked Celia, and she said 'no.' And he asked Katie, and she said 'no.' And then he came to me and I had to say 'yes.' "

Tacy began to sob.

"Papa said he was amazed and astounded. He said he thought he had brought us up to appreciate good literature. He said there was a set of Dickens in the house, and Shakespeare, and Father Finn, and how did a child of his happen to be reading trash? Then he went out to the kitchen range and lifted the lid and threw it in . . ."

"Tacy!"

"Yes, he did!" wept Tacy. "And now what am I going to tell Rena?"

What, indeed!

Looking down from the maple, Betsy could see Rena contentedly stringing beans on the back doorstep, unconscious of her loss. Rena had come from a farm to help Mrs. Ray. She was young and good-natured, not like Tib's mother's hired girl, Matilda, who was old and cross. But even Rena got mad sometimes, and her paper-backed novels were her dearest treasures. She kept them locked in her trunk, and Betsy read them out loud to her evenings when Mr. and Mrs. Ray happened to be out—at their High Fly Whist Club or a lodge dance or prayer meeting. Prompted by the same instinct that had caused Tacy to hide *Lady Audley's Secret* under her bed, Betsy had never mentioned these readings to her father and mother. But she had told all the stories to Tacy and Tib and had even persuaded Rena to lend them the books. And now *Lady Audley's Secret* had perished in the flames!

"We'll have to buy her another one," said Betsy. "They have those paper-backed books at Cook's Book Store. I've seen them."

"But they cost a dime," answered Tacy through her tears.

That was true. And a dime, ten cents, was hard to come by, especially when one could not tell for what one needed it.

"We'll earn it," said Betsy stoutly.

"How?" asked Tacy.

"Somehow. You'll see."

"Betsy! Tacy!" came a voice from below.

4

"It's Tib," said Betsy. "Come on up," she called. And in half a minute a fluff of yellow hair rose into view. Tib swung herself lightly to a seat on a neighboring branch.

Tib had been friends with Betsy and Tacy almost as long as they had been friends with each other. She lived two blocks away on Pleasant Street in a large chocolate-colored house. Betsy's house faced Tacy's at the end of Hill Street. The town ended and the country began there, on a green tree-covered hill that made a beautiful playground for all the neighborhood children. There was hardly a day when Tib did not come to play with Betsy and Tacy.

She looked anxiously now at Tacy's tear-stained face.

"What's the matter?" she asked.

"Tacy's father found *Lady Audley's Secret* under her bed."

"And he threw it in the kitchen stove," said Tacy. "He said it was trash."

"Trash!" cried Betsy. "I'm trying to write books just like it."

Tib's round blue eyes grew rounder.

"What are you going to tell Rena?" she asked.

"We're not going to tell her anything," said Betsy, "until we have a dime to buy her another book."

"How are you going to get a dime?" asked Tib.

"We're going to earn it," said Betsy. "But we haven't quite decided how."

The screen door creaked, and they looked down to see Rena with the pan of beans under her arm going into the kitchen. At the same moment they saw something else. . . . Julia, with a boy beside her, walking up Hill Street.

5

Julia was fourteen. Her skirt came down to the tops of her shoes. A braid with a curl on the end hung down her back, past her slender, belted waist. She wore a big hat.

The boy, who wore the uniform of a military school, was carrying her books.

"It's a good thing," said Betsy sarcastically, "that she has Jerry to carry those heavy books."

"They'd break her back practically," said Tacy, "if she had to carry them herself."

"Look at him help her up the steps!" jeered Betsy. "It's too bad she's so weak."

"This going around with boys makes me sick," said Tacy.

"I like Herbert Humphreys," said Tib.

It was just like Tib to like a boy and say so.

"Oh, if you have to have a boy around, it might as well be Herbert," said Betsy, who liked him too.

"He wears cute clothes," said Tacy, blushing.

Herbert Humphreys, who had come to Deep Valley from St. Paul, wore knickerbockers. The other boys in their grade wore plain short pants.

"Why does Jerry wear a uniform?" asked Tib, peering down.

"He goes away to school. To Cox Military. It hasn't opened yet. And every day he walks up to the high school to walk home with Julia. Silly!" Betsy gave a sniff. "But he's nice. I'll say that much. He's mighty nice to me. Always giving me money for candy . . . Tacy!" She broke off in a shout. "Money! A dime! Ten cents!"

"Of course," cried Tacy, a smile breaking over her face.

"What is it? What are you talking about?" asked Tib in bewilderment.

"We need money, don't we?" asked Betsy. "Well, here's our chance to earn some."

"But how?" demanded Tib, as Betsy swung downward.

"By being nuisances," cried Tacy, following.

"Do you get *paid* for being nuisances?"

"For not being nuisances."

"I don't understand."

Betsy hung to a limb to explain.

"Jerry likes to talk to Julia without us sticking around. So sometimes he gives us money to go to the store for candy."

"Oh," said Tib, and slid nimbly to the ground.

Down on the ground, Tib did not look to be ten, much less her actual age of twelve. She was dainty and small. With her short yellow hair, round eyes and rosebud mouth, she looked like a doll. She wore a long-waisted pink lawn dress and a pink bow in her hair. Betsy and Tacy wore sailor suits.

Betsy was not so tall as Tacy but she was taller than she had been at ten. She wore her brown braids crossed in back and tied with perky ribbons which somehow matched her perky smiling face.

Tacy was slim and long of limb. Her face was still crowded with freckles, but they didn't matter when she shook back her curls and looked out shyly with blue Irish eyes.

All three were barefoot.

Single file they padded softly around the corner of the yellow cottage. A vine was turning red over the small front porch. Julia sat in the hammock there and Jerry sat on the

7

railing staring into her slim wistful face.

"Why does he look at her like that? She's only Julia," Tacy whispered.

"Don't ask *me*," answered Betsy in disgust.

"Why does Julia look so sad?" asked Tib.

"She's just putting that look on. Thinks it's pretty," Betsy said. Scornfully she led the way to the porch.

Jerry turned around and smiled. He had a friendly, toothy smile in a brown pleasant face.

"Hello, kids," he said.

"Hello, children," said Julia languidly.

"*Kids! Children!*" said Betsy, not quite under her breath.

"Hello," said Tacy.

"Hello," said Tib.

They sat down in a row on the steps.

Conversation on the porch lagged. Julia unpinned her hat and fluffed her dark pompadour. She wore a big bow on the top of her head and another at the top of her braid.

"Remember, Jerry," she said at last, "you promised to help me with my algebra."

"Glad to," Jerry said.

"Betsy," said Julia. "I think mamma is looking for you."

"She can't be," said Betsy. "She's taken Margaret down town to get an English bob."

"Maybe Rena is looking for you then," said Julia pointedly.

"Nobody's looking for me," said Betsy.

"Or me either," said Tacy.

"Or me either," said Tib.

They sat like lumps.

"Algebra," said Julia, "is hard. Jerry can't explain it with so many around. He can't concentrate."

"That's right," said Jerry. He turned around to smile at them again. Betsy liked him when he smiled. But she hardened her heart and didn't budge.

"Oh, well," said Julia. "Let's let the arithmetic go. Come on in the house, Jerry, and sing a while. I have some of the music from *Robin Hood*. Did you hear it?"

"Yes, I did."

"Wasn't it good? I went with papa and mamma. They decided I was old enough to start going to the theatre and they thought *Robin Hood* was a good thing to begin on. I loved it. I'm sure I'll like grand opera better, though."

Betsy writhed. It was her sorest grievance that she had not seen *Robin Hood*. She had never even been inside the Opera House.

Chatting in a grown-up way, Julia went into the house and Jerry followed. Betsy and Tacy and Tib followed too. They sat down in the largest, most comfortable chairs. They said nothing.

Julia went to the piano stool and ran her white fingers trippingly over the keys. She fluttered the music on the rack.

"Here's that good baritone solo. Sing it for me, Jerry."

"Well, gosh!" said Jerry, bending to look at it. "I'd like to. But I'm no De Wolf Hopper."

"Please, Jerry! You've sung for me before."

"But we were alone."

Julia turned the piano stool about.

"Why don't you three run over to Kelly's to play?" she asked pleadingly.

"Paul's got the stomach ache," said Tacy. "Too many green apples."

"Mamma's got company," said Tib, after being nudged.

"I'm afraid we've got to stay right here," said Betsy. "Of course," she added cautiously after a moment, "we could go to Mrs. Chubbock's store for candy . . . if we had any money."

"We haven't any though," said Tacy. "At least I haven't."

"Neither have I," said Tib.

"Neither have I," said Betsy. "Not a cent."

Jerry dived into his pocket.

"Here, take this," he said, pulling out a dime.

Betsy looked from the dime to Tacy. And Tacy looked from the dime to Betsy. And Tib looked from the dime to Betsy and Tacy. What they were thinking, of course, was, "Of all the luck!" But Jerry misunderstood.

"Maybe a dime isn't enough," he said, "for three of you. Of course it isn't! You need a nickel apiece."

And he drew out a nickel.

This time Betsy and Tacy and Tib did not hesitate. With shouted thanks they grabbed and ran. They ran to Tacy's hitching block.

"There's enough for the book and *still* some for candy!"

"A nickel's worth of jaw-breakers!"

"Let's go down town right now," suggested Betsy. "We can go to Cook's Book Store and buy the book. Get some jaw-breakers on the way. Of course, we'll have to ask."

"Mamma will let us go, I think," said Tacy. "She feels sorry for me, on account of how hard I cried. Wait here while I ask."

She ran into the house.

She was slow in returning, but when she came it was with a sparkling face.

"We may go if we put on shoes and stockings. I've put mine on."

"Mine are underneath the maple," said Tib, darting off.

"I'll get mine," Betsy said.

She raced into the house and upstairs to the little front bedroom. She and Julia shared it with Margaret now. Rena slept in the little back bedroom that had once been Margaret's. The house was getting crowded, Mr. Ray said.

11

Rena was baking gingerbread. Betsy could tell by the smell rising from the kitchen. In the parlor Jerry was singing a song about *Brown October Ale*.

Betsy and Tacy and Tib started down Hill Street. They were pleased and excited because they were going down town. But they did not suspect what marvel they would see before they returned.

II

THE HORSELESS CARRIAGE

THE walk down town was uneventful . . . as uneventful as a walk down town could be. It always seemed important to go beyond Lincoln Park, that pie-shaped wedge of lawn with an elm tree and a fountain on it which marked the end of the neighborhood.

Ahead stretched Broad Street where fine houses sat on wide, tree-shaded streets. Wooden sidewalks changed to cement ones here. Church steeples loomed ahead, and the shiny framework of the new Carnegie Library.

"When that library is finished," Betsy remarked, "we won't need to borrow our novels from Rena."

Parallel with Broad Street to the right were other streets rising one above another on the bluff. The High School that Julia and Katie attended lifted its tower there.

Parallel with Broad Street to the left was Second Street with more houses, churches, livery stables, and the Opera House. Beyond that, Front Street lay along the river. But the river could not be seen except in glimpses between stores and shops, the Depot, the Big Mill, and Mr. Melborn Poppy's splendid Melborn Hotel.

September lay upon Front Street in pale golden light. Horses were drowsing at hitching rings and poles. In front of the Lion Department Store a bronze lion stood guard over a drinking trough. The thoroughfare was quiet, except for the occasional clop clop of horses on the paving and the whir of passing bicycles.

"Let's get our jaw-breakers first," said Tib, so they went into Schulte's Grocery Store and bought a nickel's worth of jaw-breakers. They divided them equally and went on to Cook's Book Store.

"A copy of *Lady Audley's Secret*, please," said Betsy, putting down their dime.

Mr. Cook looked at them sharply out of very bright blue eyes. He was tall and thin and wore a toupee, thick and silky, parted in the middle.

"That is a strange book for three little girls to be buying," he remarked.

"We're buying it for my mother's hired girl," said Betsy. "She likes those ten-cent books."

"It's a fine story, Mr. Cook," volunteered Tib, and Betsy and Tacy both nudged her. They didn't think it was such a good idea to let Mr. Cook know that they read Rena's novels. But he accepted their dime.

It was when they came out of the store, with *Lady Audley's Secret* under Tacy's arm, that they had their first hint of the marvel which was to make the day forever memorable.

Front Street was suddenly full of people. People seemed to have sprung up from nowhere, and all were rushing in one direction as though blown by a great wind. Shoppers; clerks from stores, wearing alpaca jackets; hatless women, untying aprons as they went; dozens and dozens of children.

"Whatever can it be? What's happened?"

Betsy, Tacy, and Tib started to run.

They sighted Winona Root, pedaling by on her bicycle. She was a classmate who lived on School Street in a white-painted brick house with a terrace and a beautiful garden. Her father was the editor of the *Deep Valley Sun*.

Winona had black hair that hung in long straight locks on either side of a somewhat sallow face. She had gleaming black eyes and very white teeth which she showed almost constantly in a teasing smile. She always wore bright dresses of red, purple or yellow. She was wearing a purple one now.

"Winona! Stop! Tell us what's the matter!"

"Don't you know?"

"If we did, we wouldn't ask you."

Winona grinned.

"Don't you wish you *did* know?"

"Of course. Please tell us, Winona."

Winona stopped pedaling. She rested on long legs.

"Well," she said, drawing out the suspense. "It came this noon but he's just got it to going."

"Who is 'he' and what is 'it'?"

"*He* is Mr. Poppy who owns the Melborn Hotel and runs the Opera House. *It* is down by the Opera House now."

"But what *is* 'it'? Winona Root, you tell us. You might as well! We'll follow the crowd and find out."

"All right," said Winona, not wanting to be cheated of the pleasure of delivering the news. "It's a horseless carriage."

A horseless carriage! Betsy, Tacy, and Tib were stunned into silence.

There had been rumors for some time of a marvelous invention called the horseless carriage, a vehicle that ran without being pushed or pulled . . . even uphill. They had seen pictures of it. *The Ladies' Home Journal* had shown Miss Julia Marlowe, the actress, sitting in one. And some Deep Valley people had gone to the Twin Cities, as Minneapolis and St. Paul are called in Minnesota, to view the wonder. But this was the first automobile to reach Deep Valley.

Winona took their silence for skepticism.

"Come on, if you don't believe me. My father's going to have a ride in it, so's he can write a piece for the paper. I'll be the first kid in town to get a ride, I imagine."

She probably would be, Betsy thought gloomily. Winona Root did everything first. Just because her father was an editor, she had complimentary tickets—'comps,' they were called—to the circus, to the Dog and Pony Show, to the glass blowers, to the lantern slide performances, to all the matinees that played at the Opera House.

"Maybe you won't be," said Tib.

"Betcha I will," Winona answered.

She jumped on her bicycle and started pedaling with long agile legs. Betsy, Tacy, and Tib raced along behind her.

"I don't even want to be," panted Tacy as she ran.

"Want to be what?"

"The first to get a ride. I'd be scared."

"What of?" asked Tib.

"The horseless carriage. It sounds crazy to me. If there isn't a horse to say 'whoa!' to, how do you stop the thing?"

"That's what I wonder," said Betsy. "How does it know when Mr. Poppy is ready to stop?"

"It might keep right on going."

"Up one street and down another."

"Into the slough, maybe."

"Or into the river."

"Are you scared too?" Tib asked Betsy.

"Well . . . Winona Root can have the first ride for all of me."

"I'm not scared," said Tib. "I'd like to be the first to ride."

They ran past the office in which Tacy's father sold sewing machines; it was closed. Past Ray's Shoe Store; that was closed too. Store after store was closed and empty. They reached the Melborn Hotel and turned the corner and ran to the Opera House.

There, where the crowd was thickest, they could see what looked like an open carriage . . . only without any shafts and without a horse hitched to it. Near by stood Mr. Root and Winona, the Mayor and other notables, and, of course, the Poppys.

Mr. and Mrs. Poppy were worth looking at themselves when there wasn't a horseless carriage about. He weighed over three hundred pounds and his wife, two-thirds as much. Today they looked even larger than usual, for they wore the loose linen dusters fashionable for automobiling. Mr. Poppy wore a leather cap that had flaps tied over his ears and enormous froglike goggles. Mrs. Poppy's hat was tied down with yards and yards of veiling.

The Poppys were always models of elegance. They were city people; they had come from Minneapolis, and no one in town knew them very well. They lived in the hotel; Mrs. Poppy did not keep house as other Deep Valley wives did. Blonde and radiant, she was said to look like the famous beauty and actress, Lillian Russell . . . except that she was stouter, of course. Before her marriage, she had been an actress herself.

She and her husband went to the Twin Cities often, to see plays. But they saw plays in Deep Valley too. When Mr. Poppy built the Opera House, he had two special seats made for Mrs. Poppy and himself. Extra wide, extra deep, and extra comfortable, designed for extra-stout people. Betsy had heard about them often.

She and Tacy and Tib squirmed through the crowd until

they were near the Poppys. A sweet scent floated from Mrs. Poppy, and whenever she moved there was silken rustle beneath the linen duster. She looked down to smile at Tib. Tib always drew a flattering smile even from strangers; and today in the long-waisted pink lawn dress, she looked even prettier than usual.

A man in overalls lay underneath the horseless carriage. Wrenches and other tools were scattered in the dust.

"Two hours' work for one hour's riding is the average, I hear," the Mayor remarked jocularly to Mr. Poppy.

"Oh, come now! It isn't that bad," answered Mr. Poppy, smiling too, although his round red face with its garlands of chins looked hot and flustered. "How you coming, Jim?" he called to the man underneath the carriage.

The man crawled out. He was Sunny Jim who worked in the livery stable next door to the Opera House. Everyone called him Sunny Jim because of his resemblance to the smiling figure in the Force advertisements.

"It'll go this time, sir. No doubt about it."

Mr. Poppy turned with a courtly bow to his wife.

"First ride for Mrs. Poppy. And then you gentlemen must try it out."

Winona took her father's hand.

"May I go along, father?" she asked.

"We'll see," her father answered indulgently.

Winona grinned wickedly at Tib.

There was a spreading circle of perfume and a swishing sound of silken petticoats as Mr. Poppy handed Mrs. Poppy

into the back seat. Settling herself comfortably, she almost filled it. Under her veil-tied hat, her face glowed with pleasure.

"You show commendable courage, Mrs. Poppy," said Winona's father, leaning forward.

"Oh, I adore automobiling," Mrs. Poppy answered.

She smiled at the crowd, and her smile lingered on the group of children. She and Mr. Poppy were very fond of children although they had none of their own. Tib waved at her, and Mrs. Poppy waved gloved fingers in response.

"Steady now," Mr. Poppy said.

He walked to the back of the vehicle and turned a crank. With Sunny Jim at his elbow and the crowd waiting intently, he turned it again . . . and again. He turned it once again, and there was an explosive chugging noise. The carriage began to shake.

"Good!" cried Mr. Poppy, and he ran around and climbed into the front seat where the children now observed a wheel at the right side. He took this into his hands with firm determination. The carriage continued to shake convulsively. An evil smell crept into the air.

Sunny Jim rushed to Mr. Poppy's side. He shouted excited directions. Mr. Poppy turned keys, pressed pedals, pulled levers. The carriage was shaking so hard now that Mrs. Poppy vibrated like jelly, but she continued to smile.

"Got it, Mr. Poppy?" Sunny Jim shouted.

"Got it."

"Off, sir?"

"Well, practically."

And at that sovereign moment, Tib danced forward.

"Please, Mr. Poppy," she called. "May I have a ride?"

Betsy gasped, and Tacy gulped. They had not dreamed that Tib had this in mind. It would be an inconceivable glory to get the first ride. What a triumph over Winona Root!

But Mr. Poppy was too busy turning keys, pressing pedals, and pulling levers even to glance at Tib.

"Some other time, little girl! Some other time!" he answered absently.

Winona Root flashed Betsy and Tacy a smile of good-natured scorn.

Mrs. Poppy leaned forward to touch her husband's shoulder.

"Give her a ride, Mel. She can sit here with me and won't be a bit of trouble."

"All right . . . if you want her."

"Come along, dear. Jump up!"

Mrs. Poppy moved heavily over, drawing aside her billowing fragrant skirts. Tib jumped.

"Father!" Winona Root called urgently. "Can't I . . ."

But it was too late. With a burst of vapor and a clanking that drowned out her voice, the horseless carriage moved. It actually moved. It went ahead without pushing or pulling. It ran right along behind nothing.

The crowd sent up a tremendous cheer. Betsy and Tacy yelled at the tops of their voices. Nestled beneath Mrs. Poppy's bosom, Tib waved frantically to Betsy and Tacy who waved frantically back.

Horses reared, and drivers all around pulled at their reins.

23

The crowd ran along beside the uncannily moving vehicle. Betsy caught a glimpse of her father . . . he was throwing his hat into the air. For just a moment he did not look like her father; he looked like a boy. She saw Tacy's father, too; and Tib's. And Herbert Humphreys, wearing his knickerbockers. And Tom Slade. And ever so many of their schoolmates. All were running madly beside the horseless carriage.

But it gained speed. It left them behind. Clanking, rattling, spitting, it turned the corner and vanished from sight.

Betsy and Tacy jumped up and down and screamed a while. Then they raced back to the Opera House. In the milling crowd they found Winona Root, standing under one of the two billboards that flanked the entrance doors. Her teeth gleamed in her indomitable smile.

"Yah! Yah!" yelled Betsy and Tacy. "Tib got the first ride!"

"What of it?"

"What of it?" shouted Betsy indignantly. "You said *you* were going to be the first. That's what!"

Winona flipped a careless arm toward the advertisement above her.

"See that? *Uncle Tom's Cabin* or *Life Among the Lowly*. They're giving a matinee next Saturday. I'm going."

"What of it?" Tacy remembered to retort. But Betsy's gaze wandered to the billboard and clung there fascinated.

"I've read the book," said Betsy slowly.

" 'Foremost American drama and the nation's pride,' " Winona read aloud. " 'Dear to Americans as the Declaration of Independence. Struck the death knell of slavery.' "

24

"Pooh!" said Tacy.

" 'Presenting America's most talented and beautiful child actress, Miss Evelyn Montmorency, in the role of Little Eva,' " chanted Winona. " 'Don't miss her ascension to the heavenly gates, nor the grand brilliant spectacular transformation scene.' "

"She dies and goes to Heaven," Betsy said.

" 'See the ferocious pack of man-eating Siberian bloodhounds. See them chase Eliza in the most thrilling scene ever depicted!' "

"They chase her over the ice," Betsy explained. "She jumps from block to block."

" 'Hear the plantation singers! See the comical Topsy do her famous breakdown dance! See the heart-breaking, tear-wringing death of Uncle Tom . . .' "

"I've heard that on the graphophone!" Tacy interrupted excitedly. "You've heard it, Betsy! The flogging scene . . ."

Winona Root looked from one to the other, smiling exultantly. Reaching into her pocket, she pulled out four pieces of pasteboard, and held them above her head.

" 'Comps!' " she said. "Four of them! I asked my father for them and I got them, just a minute ago. I can take three kids but I haven't quite decided which ones I will take."

With an impish grin, Winona sprang to her bicycle.

A clanking and rattling was heard up the street.

"Here it comes!" "Here it comes!" "Here's the horseless carriage back again!"

The crowd shouted, and Betsy and Tacy shouted louder than anyone. But Winona did not wait to see Tib's triumph. Flourishing her tickets in an upflung arm, guiding herself with one jaunty hand, she pedaled off toward home.

The horseless carriage drew to a stop exactly in front of the Opera House.

"You see," Betsy said. "Mr. Poppy knows how to stop it."

Tib stepped out, smiling.

"Thank you, Mr. Poppy. Thank you, Mrs. Poppy," she said politely. She flung a glance toward Herbert Humphreys, who was staring in admiration, and danced away to join Betsy and Tacy.

Tib was modest about her sensational ride; Tib was always

modest. But as they walked up Front Street, up Broad Street, up Hill Street, going home with Rena's book, she told them exactly how it felt to ride in a horseless carriage.

"It's grand," she said. "No old horse in front to block your view. You simply sail along. And you can go so *fast*. Twelve miles in an hour, Mr. Poppy said. Of course, we only went ten today, because we were in town and the horses were so scared."

"Were *you* scared?" Tacy asked.

"Not a bit."

Then Betsy and Tacy told her about the coming of *Uncle Tom's Cabin*. They told her about Little Eva and Topsy, the transformation scene and the flogging scene and Eliza crossing the ice. They told her about Winona's tickets to the Saturday matinee.

"Gee whiz!" said Betsy. "We've just *got* to be the ones she takes."

"I'd certainly like to see those man-eating blood hounds," said Tib.

"I'd have to keep my eyes closed while they flogged Uncle Tom though," said Tacy, the tender-hearted.

"I want to see Little Eva go up to Heaven. She goes right up while you're watching her, and sits on a pink cloud. It's spiffy," Betsy said. "How *can* we make her ask us?"

"We've got to manage it somehow."

"We've just *got* to!"

But before they thought of a way to inveigle an invitation out of Winona Root, they met Jerry. He was walking down

Hill Street whistling the song about *Brown October Ale*.

"There's a horseless carriage in town!" Betsy, Tacy, and Tib shouted together.

"I rode in it!"

"Tib rode in it!"

"No!" Jerry cried. "Whose is it? Where is it? Gosh, I'm crazy to see one." He set off at a run down town.

And Betsy, Tacy, and Tib savored again the triumph of Tib's ride. They progressed up Hill Street slowly, pausing at every house to shout the news. They collected a crowd of envious children, of agitated women.

"It's grand," Tib repeated over and over again. "You sail right along behind nothing."

III

WINONA'S TICKETS

NEXT morning on the way to school they held an earnest consultation on the matter of getting Winona Root to invite them to *Uncle Tom's Cabin.*

The evening had gone with much jubilant talk of Tib's ride in the horseless carriage. At the Ray supper table, at the Kelly supper table, at the Muller supper table, in Rena's and Matilda's kitchens and, later, on the Rays' hitching block surrounded by spellbound children in the smoky September dusk, Betsy, Tacy, and Tib had told and retold the afternoon's adventure. Even modest Tib had swaggered a little as she tripped down Hill Street on her homeward way.

In the morning, however, she was the one to suggest that hereafter they should belittle her achievement.

"We mustn't brag in front of Winona. She'd give those tickets away right in front of our face and eyes."

"That's right, Tib. You're smart to think of that."

"Well, we've bragged plenty anyway," Betsy said contentedly. "Even Julia was just knocked over by your ride."

"So was Katie," Tacy said. "And my big brothers! They made me tell them every single thing you said, Tib."

With a long satisfied sigh, Tib dismissed her honors.

"Let's plan now how to go after those tickets. I've got an idea."

Tib's idea was a practical one, of course. Tib was always practical. She proposed to bribe Winona Root with a combined gift of all their treasures. Betsy's agate marble, Tacy's copy of a Gibson Girl, her own Schlitz beer calendar, sent by her uncle in Milwaukee.

"She'd be sure to take us in return for all that," Tib said.

Betsy, however, favored acting as though they didn't want to go.

"She's so contrary. She's most apt to invite us if we act as though we didn't care a thing about it."

Tacy disagreed.

"I think we ought to be extra nice to her. Ask her to play at recess. Ask her to come home to play after school. Mamma bakes today, and she'd give us some bread right out of the oven, with honey on it. You could let her ride your bicycle, Tib. And Betsy could let her use the telephone."

Mr. Ray had just installed a telephone; it was a novelty to Hill Street.

"She's got a telephone herself," said Betsy. "They had the first one in town."

"Well, she can telephone her mother then."

But Betsy shook her head.

"It would be just like her to let us do all that, and then give the tickets to somebody else."

Tacy and Tib knew that this was true. All of them could visualize Winona's mocking smile.

They had reached Mrs. Chubbock's candy store beside

the school grounds when Tacy stopped suddenly and clutched an arm of either friend.

"I've got it! We'll hypnotize her!"

"Hypnotize her!"

"You remember the hypnotist who came to the Opera House last year? Mary and Celia saw him. He could make anyone do anything he wanted to, just by thinking about it. Let's us think toward Winona. '*Take* us to *Uncle Tom's Cabin. Take* us to *Uncle Tom's Cabin.*'"

"Tacy Kelly, that's wonderful!" cried Betsy.

But Tib was doubtful.

"Don't you remember," she asked, "that just after the hypnotist came, we tried to hypnotize our fathers? We tried to make them give us a dollar. We thought about it at every meal. I stared at papa just like you told me to and thought, 'Give me a dollar. Give me a dollar.' You all did the same thing, but not one of us got a dollar."

It was just like Tib to dig up this unsuccessful venture.

"Tib," said Betsy. "You forget. There was just one of us thinking toward each father. Besides, a dollar is a lot of money. If we'd made it a nickel or a penny, we'd probably have got it. All three of us will be thinking toward Winona Root, and she can't help but feel it. It will be powerful. It will be terrific."

"We can try it," Tib said glumly.

"We'll all think the same thing," said Tacy. "'*Take* us to *Uncle Tom's Cabin. Take* us. *Take* us. *Take* us.'"

"I like that," said Betsy. "It sounds like a poem. Let's practice it now."

31

They put their arms around one another's shoulders and bent their heads together.

"*Take* us to *Uncle Tom's Cabin. Take* us. *Take* us. *Take* us."

It did sound like a poem. It sounded weird and mysterious.

"We'll stare at her while we think it," said Betsy.

"That's what the hypnotist did," Tacy explained.

The school bell rang noisily, and Betsy, Tacy, and Tib ran across the sandy boys' yard and up the long flight of steps leading to the school door. They went up to the second floor and into their room.

Miss Paxton was their teacher. She had a gray pompadour and wore shirt-waist suits in which her stock was always very high and her belt very trim. The room was sunny and large. There was a bouquet of purple asters, goldenrod, and sumac leaves on Miss Paxton's tidy desk.

Betsy, Tacy, and Tib took their seats, which were not close together. Every year they sought for adjoining seats and every year the teacher foiled their plan and placed them as far apart as possible. Betsy and Tacy sat toward the back of the room, one at the far right and one at the far left. Tib sat near the front. Winona Root sat halfway back in the very center of the room.

With the second bell she dashed in, wearing a red dress. Her black eyes went at once to Tib. Tib was staring at her. Winona seated herself with a breezy flipping of skirts. Tib turned around and continued to stare with eyes like round moons.

Winona looked surprised. She had expected bragging,

boasting, taunts, perhaps. But not this . . . whatever it was. Slightly uncomfortable, she turned to the left, only to find Tacy's Irish eyes fixed on her dreamily. She turned to the right and encountered Betsy's piercing hazel gaze.

Winona tossed her head.

Miss Paxton called for "Position." She smiled at Tib.

"You may pick the opening song, Thelma," she said. "That is, if you will turn around and face the front."

Tib picked, *"Onward Christian Soldiers."* And she turned around and faced the front, but only for a moment. When the singing began, she twisted about to stare at Winona. Betsy and Tacy were staring at her too. Betsy was not singing the right words of the hymn. She was singing (but softly, so that no one could hear):

> *"Take* us, *take* us, *take* us,
> Take us to the show,
> *Take* us, *take* us, *take* us,
> To Uncle Tom, you know."

After the hymn came the prayer. Betsy and Tacy consulted with their eyes as to whether it would be sinful to hypnotize while praying. Deciding that it wouldn't be, they put their hands over their eyes reverently but stared through their fingers at their victim. Tib, when she saw what they were doing, did the same.

After the prayer came physical exercises. Tom was asked to open all the windows, and the boys and girls stood and jerked their arms up and down, out and back, in time to Miss Paxton's "One, two. One, two."

Betsy jerked her arms in time to, *"Take* us. *Take* us." She mouthed the words to Tacy who began to say them too. Both of them stared unceasingly at Winona. Tib turned around to stare.

"Face *front*, Thelma," Miss Paxton interrupted her counting to cry.

Reluctantly Tib faced front.

When the class sat down, Miss Paxton folded her hands on the desk. She looked around brightly.

"I heard some interesting news this morning," she said. "A member of our class, Thelma Muller, had a ride in the new automobile that reached town yesterday."

She smiled at Tib. But Tib looked blank.

"Did you enjoy it?" Miss Paxton asked.

"It was all right," said Tib.

"Would you like to come up front and tell us about it?"

"There's nothing to tell, Miss Paxton," Tib replied.

Miss Paxton looked crestfallen, and also surprised. Tib was anything but shy. Usually she enjoyed an opportunity to appear before the class. Winona looked mystified too, and Betsy and Tacy, whom Miss Paxton had expected to see puffed up with pride, were yawning.

"In that case," said Miss Paxton, to end an awkward pause, "we will study geography."

With a series of thuds and bangs, the big geography books were brought out and opened. Quiet descended on the room. Stealthily, Tib took a sideways pose again. Instead of looking at the New England states, she looked at Winona.

Tacy sat turned to the right. Her face framed by her long red curls, she gazed fervently at Winona. Betsy sat turned

34

to the left. Leaning on one elbow, she stared at Winona too.

Winona shifted uneasily. She looked around once or twice.

"Now," said Miss Paxton, "you may close your books. Betsy, will you name the New England states?"

Betsy jumped up.

"*Take* us. *Take* us. *Take* us," she began.

"What did you say?" Miss Paxton asked sharply.

"Excuse me, Miss Paxton. That was a mistake. Maine, New Hampshire, Vermont . . ."

Next they studied arithmetic. Again Tib studied half turned around.

"Thelma," said Miss Paxton, "I don't know what's got

into you today. Please face the front and look at your book instead of at Winona."

Tib flung Betsy and Tacy a pleading look. She turned to the front. Betsy and Tacy kept on staring. Winona was like a mouse between two cats.

At recess Betsy and Tacy and Tib sat with their backs to the high board fence that marked off the girls' yard. Their legs were stuck out stiff and straight in front of them. They sat motionless, staring at Winona.

She was playing Prisoners' Base, and whenever she flashed past them on long jaunty legs, she glanced quickly to see whether they were staring. They always were.

The bell rang and the children crowded into line. Winona pulled four tickets from the pocket of her dress.

" 'Comps,' " she said, tossing her black locks. "They're for *Uncle Tom's Cabin.* I've got three to give away."

She turned around to see whether Betsy and Tacy and Tib were listening. They were. They were listening, and they were staring with marble-like eyes. Their lips were moving soundlessly.

After recess came the reading lesson. While the others, in turn, droned through *The Courtship of Miles Standish,* Betsy, Tacy, and Tib stared at Winona.

"Thelma Muller, you are to look toward the *front*," Miss Paxton said.

"Tacy Kelly. Please sit straight in your seat. You aren't looking toward the front either."

"Betsy Ray. Look toward the *front*. What ails you three today?"

Beneath her desk, Winona got out the tickets. She spread them into a fan; she built a little house with them; she showed them to the boy in front of her and to the girl behind. Now and then she glanced at Betsy, Tacy, and Tib with nervous bravado.

At last the bell announced that it was time for the noon departure. Miss Paxton rapped on her desk.

"Position! Rise! Turn! March!"

The grade formed into two lines and marched into the hall, but even in this orderly procession Tib turned around to stare. Betsy leaned out from her place in line to stare, and so did Tacy. Glances like bullets shot toward Winona.

Winona brought out her tickets again. She flourished them defiantly.

" 'Comps,' " she called to Herbert Humphreys in the boys' line. "For *Uncle Tom's Cabin*. Don't you wish you were me?"

"Who're you taking, Winona?" Herbert Humphreys asked.

"I haven't decided," said Winona. Her teeth gleamed wickedly. She looked down the line toward Betsy and up the line toward Tib.

They were staring of course. They were staring harder than they had ever stared before. Their eyes were almost popping from their heads with their agonized concentration.

"I know who I *won't* take," Winona said loudly.

"Who?" Herbert Humphreys asked.

"People who stare at me all the time," Winona said.

She put the tickets back into her pocket.

IV

MORE ABOUT WINONA'S TICKETS

ETSY, Tacy, and Tib scarcely spoke, going home at noon.

"It didn't work," Tib said, blaming no one, just stating a fact.

"No. It didn't work," admitted Tacy.

"We won't try to hypnotize her any more," said Betsy.

That was all they said. They parted with unhappy nods.

After dinner they walked back to school still unsmiling. During the afternoon they were quiet and subdued. Tib faced toward the front, and none of them looked at Winona. Even when she counted her tickets and made a little pack of them and flipped it in all directions, they did not look at her except out of the corners of their eyes.

After school they went to Tacy's house because Mrs. Kelly was baking. It was a sight to see the plump loaves of golden brown bread pulled from the oven and buttered. Mrs. Kelly took the loaves out of their pans and set them on a clean cloth to butter them. Betsy's mouth watered when the butter melted and ran in rich streams down the nutlike crusts of the loaves. When the bread was cool enough to cut, Mrs. Kelly gave a soft piece to each of them. She gave one to Paul who ran in from the bonfire he was tending. And she gave one to Katie who was helping her as usual. Katie always helped her mother after school these days. Mary and Celia were typewriter girls now and away from home all day. Katie was as cheerful about work as though it were play. She seemed to like helping her mother with the bread.

Betsy and Tacy and Tib began to feel better when they had buttered their bread and spread honey on it and gone out to the pump in Tacy's back yard. This was a favorite place with them. The wooden platform made a comfortable seat, and they could look up at the encircling hills where the softwood trees were turning red and yellow, making bright bouquets against the green. Smoke from Paul's bon-

fire scented the air that was as warm and golden as their bread.

Betsy had been thinking deeply about *Uncle Tom's Cabin.* Her heart yearned toward the play as it had never yearned toward anything before. The longing was a little like what she felt when she saw rows and rows of books in other people's bookcases. (She had read all the books in the bookcase at home.) But this feeling was stronger and more violent. She *had* to go to *Uncle Tom's Cabin!* She *had* to!

It was more than possible that if she asked her father, he would let her go. But then, what about Tacy? Tacy's father ruled his kingdom of children with a kindly but inflexible justice. What one child had, all of them had, or its equivalent. What one child did, all of them did. He would not send Tacy to a matinee at the Opera House unless he could afford to send Katie and Paul too. As for Tib, she might not be allowed to go. Tib's mother was strict. And for Betsy to see *Uncle Tom's Cabin* without Tacy or Tib would be a hollow joy.

If all three were invited to go as Winona's guests, the situation would be different. That would be a party; they could accept, of course. Somehow the three of them had to be invited. But Betsy was empty of ideas.

Tib was hopeful that the matter could be arranged.

"Let's try my plan," she said, "of telling her we want to go and offering her presents."

"No," said Betsy. "At least, let's not say right out that we want to go. If we do that, and she doesn't take us, she can laugh at us. We might give her the presents though, in a careless kind of way."

"Let's do what I suggested," said Tacy. "Ask her to play after school. And while we're being nice to her, just hand out a few presents."

"All right," Betsy said. "I certainly hope it works."

They jumped up then to help Paul with the bonfire. Tib's brothers, Freddie and Hobbie, and Margaret and the Rivers' children were helping him too. Paul's black and brown mongrel dog, Gyp, was rushing about through the leaves. The children threw sticks which he retrieved with happy snorts. They had a good time, but through it all Betsy thought with longing about *Uncle Tom's Cabin*.

At recess the next day she said to Winona, "Come on and play with us."

"Let's play statues," said Tacy. "I always think you're good at statues, Winona."

"You can make such awful faces," said Tib.

Winona looked suspicious but flattered.

"All right," she said, and they played statues. When Tacy flung Winona, she called out "Cross schoolteacher!" And Winona's scowling face between locks of black hair, her fiercely upraised finger were pronounced magnificent.

"You're practically an actress, Winona," Betsy said. "It's probably because you go to so many plays."

"You're certainly lucky," said Tacy.

"I should say you are," said Tib.

The bell rang, and Betsy said, "Why don't you come home with us after school? You've never been to see us. We could have lots of fun."

Winona's eyes glittered with dawning comprehension.

"All right," she replied. "I'd just as soon."

Winona enjoyed herself that afternoon. They went to Betsy's house first and urged Winona to telephone her mother over the Rays' new telephone. It was fixed into the wall beside the dining-room door. Winona had to climb on a stool to reach it. She rang the bell, lifted the receiver and said "Hello Central" with an assurance that her companions envied. Her mother was surprised to hear from her.

Afterwards they played a game of ping pong. (Winona's side won, of course.) They took her out in the kitchen and introduced her to Rena, red cheeked and pretty with ribbons woven into the braid that was knotted behind her pompadour. Rena gave them some rocks she had baked that morning. These were little cakes full of raisins and nuts and were very good.

Betsy put the agate marble secretly into her pocket. They crossed the street to Tacy's house.

There they made Gyp do his tricks for Winona. He fetched and carried willingly. They showed Winona Tacy's father's violin. And Mrs. Kelly, who did not know that they had had rocks over at the Rays', gave them some fat ginger cookies. Tacy slipped upstairs for her Gibson Girl picture. She had traced it and colored it and framed it in passe-partout. She put it under her skirt, and they all went on to Tib's house.

Tib offered Winona a ride on her bicycle. Winona had a bicycle of her own, of course, but she enjoyed riding Tib's. They took her all over Tib's beautiful house. As they came down the curving front stairs, Betsy pointed out the panes of colored glass in the entrance door. They went into the front parlor that was round because it was a tower room, and through blue velvet draperies into the back parlor where the window seat was, and through the red and gold dining room into the kitchen.

Matilda did not know they had had rocks to eat at the Rays' and ginger cookies at the Kellys'. She gave them some apple cake, and they took it out to the knoll.

While the others were eating under the oak tree, Tib skipped into the house and upstairs to her room. She came back bearing the Schlitz beer calendar that her uncle had sent her from Milwaukee. It had a picture on it of a pretty girl skating. It said, "The beer that made Milwaukee famous."

Tib looked with raised questioning eyebrows at Betsy who signaled to Tacy who nodded. Simultaneously the Schlitz beer calendar, the Gibson Girl picture, and the agate marble were thrown into Winona's lap.

"Some presents for you, Winona," Betsy said.

For just a moment Winona looked startled.

"It isn't my birthday," she said.

"Oh, we just thought you might like them," said Betsy.

"You don't come to see us very often, so we thought we'd give you some presents," said Tacy.

"That's the only reason," said Tib. "Really it is."

Winona's eyes shone now with full understanding.

"Oh," she said. "Thanks. This is a spiffy calendar. Gee, this is a good copy of a Gibson Girl. I haven't got a marble like that."

Then she jumped up.

"Well," she said. "I guess I'll have to be going."

Betsy, Tacy, and Tib looked at one another.

"Come over again," said Tib.

"What are you doing Saturday?" asked Betsy.

"Saturday?" repeated Winona. "Saturday? Oh, I remember! I'm going to *Uncle Tom's Cabin*."

"Decided who you're going to take?" asked Tacy.

"No," said Winona. "Quite a lot of people want to go. Well, good-by!"

"Good-by," said Betsy and Tacy and Tib.

They watched glumly while Winona skipped off with heartless jauntiness bearing the agate marble, the Gibson Girl picture, and the Schlitz beer calendar.

The situation was getting really desperate. This was Wednesday. Tomorrow would be Thursday. Friday was the last day before the matinee.

"Tomorrow," said Betsy. "We'll try my plan. We won't pay a bit of attention to her. Just snub her good and hard."

Tacy and Tib agreed reluctantly.

"It seems awfully dangerous," said Tacy. "Can we risk it?"

"We've got to," Betsy answered.

So the next day they snubbed Winona all day long. But it didn't help, because she didn't even notice it; she was too busy having a good time with other children who wanted to go to *Uncle Tom's Cabin*. She was decked with a thorn apple necklace that Alice had made. And she was letting everybody listen to a seashell that Herbert Humphreys' aunt had sent him from Boston, and she wore someone's gift of a peacock feather in her long black hair. When she ran at recess it floated out behind her. It suited her somehow.

She barely glanced at Betsy and Tacy and Tib. When she did look their way, it was only to see whether they were noticing her triumphs. They were.

Tib forgot her pride to ask with pretended casualness: "Decided who you're going to take to the matinee, Winona?"

"Haven't thought about it," Winona said.

She called Alice and pulled out Betsy's agate marble.

"Want to trade?" she asked.

Betsy and Tacy and Tib conferred after school in the depths of discouragement. Beside Tacy's pump they lay on their backs and looked up sadly at the glory of the hills.

"We might as well give up," said Betsy. Then in a fierce resentment of the disappointment that filled her body like an ache, she sat suddenly upright. "I know what let's do! Let's give a play ourselves."

"We often do that," said Tib. "It's fun, but it isn't like going to a play with bloodhounds in it."

"We can put bloodhounds in our play," cried Betsy. "At least we can put a dog in it. We can put Gyp in it!" Gyp heard his name and came running, leaping and barking as though stage struck.

"What play shall we give?" asked Tacy, brightening.

"I'll turn my novel into a play."

"*The Repentance of Lady Clinton?*"

"*The Repentance of Lady Clinton.* It will make a spiffy play. Before she repents, Lady Clinton gets chased by this dog. Across some chunks of ice, maybe. I haven't decided."

"If there was a girl like Topsy doing a dance," said Tib. "I could black my face and dance."

"There *is* a girl like Topsy, but I think Tacy had better play that part, because we need you for another part. There's a girl like Little Eva in it too, and she dies and goes to Heaven. We'll have to pull her up to the ceiling, and you'll be light to pull."

"How'll we manage it?"

"We'll manage. And I'll ask my mother if we can use the costumes out of Uncle Keith's trunk."

"Where shall we give this play?" asked Tib.

"Let's ask your mother if we can give it at your house. We could draw the curtains between the front and back parlors, and use the parlor for the audience to sit in, and the back parlor for the stage. We could use the dining room for a dressing room; close the sliding doors. It would be perfect."

"Do you think she'll let us?"

"We can ask her," said Tib. "Let's all go ask her now."

They bounced off the pump platform and ran down Hill Street and through the vacant lot to Tib's house.

Mrs. Muller gave her consent with surprising readiness.

"Go ahead," she said. "Matilda and I haven't house-cleaned downstairs yet. You may get those rooms good and dirty before we go to work. When do you want to give your play?"

"As soon as we can get it ready."

"The sooner, the better," Mrs. Muller said.

They raced back to the Ray house and asked Mrs. Ray whether they might use the costumes from Uncle Keith's trunk.

Uncle Keith was Mrs. Ray's brother, and no one knew where he was. Betsy had never seen him, but she had heard about him all her life.

He had run away to go on the stage when he was only seventeen. Like his sister, Betsy's mother, he was redheaded, spirited, and gay, and he had quarreled with their stepfather, a grim man who had not approved of the boy's lightheartedness. He had gone with a *Pinafore* company and had never come back. When the Spanish-American War broke out, he must have enlisted; at any rate, at just that time, his trunk came unexpectedly to Betsy's mother's house. Years had passed, but it had never been called for. And Keith had never come home.

Mrs. Ray's face shadowed when Betsy asked to use the costumes. But after a moment she smiled.

"Why not?" she said. "I can't imagine Keith objecting. And it would do the things good to be aired."

She went to the little garret off Rena's bedroom, and Rena and the children helped her pull out a flat-topped, four-square trunk.

"A real theatrical trunk," said Mrs. Ray as she unlocked it and threw back the lid.

A smell of camphor greeted twitching noses.

Betsy had seen the trunk opened before. It was always opened spring and fall at housecleaning time. But she never ceased to thrill to the depths of her being when she touched the big plumed hats, the wigs, the velvet coats.

Mrs. Ray's eyes filled with tears as she lifted out the gay trappings, but she winked and kept on smiling.

"There!" she said. "You may help me put them on the line, and after you've used them I'll pack them away again. When do you plan to give your play?"

"Next week probably," Betsy replied.

She and Tacy and Tib were so enchanted with the costumes that they almost forgot about *Uncle Tom's Cabin.* The next day, Friday, they hardly spoke to Winona. They were too busy making plans with one another. And Betsy was busy writing. She carried one of those notebooks that said on the cover: "Ray's Shoe Store. Wear Queen Quality Shoes." She wrote in it all through recess.

Winona glanced at her curiously once or twice, and at last she came close.

"How do you happen to be studying at recess?"

"I'm not studying," said Betsy.

"She's writing a play," said Tacy.

"*The Repentance of Lady Clinton,*" said Tib. "We're giving it in my parlor."

"Pooh!" said Winona. "I'm going to a real play tomorrow."

"It isn't any realer than this one is," said Betsy. "We're not charging any old pin admission, I can tell you that. We're charging five and ten cents. Ten cents for the reserved seats . . . the rocking chairs. We're going to have velvet draperies for curtains, and we're going to wear real actors' costumes."

"Where you going to get them?"

"Out of a theatrical trunk. My uncle was an actor, and we've got his trunk at home. It has tights in it, and wigs, and coats with gold braid."

Other children paused to listen. Now Betsy, Tacy, Tib, and Winona were the center of a crowd.

"Pooh!" said Winona again. "I guess you haven't any bloodhounds."

"I guess we have," said Betsy. "We're going to use Gyp . . . you saw him . . . for a bloodhound. He's going to chase Lady Clinton over cakes of ice in Tib's back parlor."

Tib shuddered. She did not know how her mother would like cakes of ice on the back-parlor carpet.

"*Is* he?" Winona demanded, turning to Tib.

"Pay a nickel, and you'll find out," Tacy cut in quickly, knowing how regrettably honest Tib was.

"That's right. If you don't believe us, just come to the show," said Tib, much relieved.

"I'm going to black my face," said Tacy, "and do my hair in pigtails."

"And I'm going to die and go to Heaven right on the stage," said Tib.

"It sounds to me," cried Winona angrily, "as though you were just copying me and having *Uncle Tom's Cabin.*"

"Well," replied Betsy. "We're not. This is a play we made up ourselves. It's called *The Repentance of Lady Clinton.*"

"Who's going to be Lady Clinton?" Winona asked.

Tib started to say, "Betsy," but at that moment she got two pokes, one from each side, one from Betsy and one from Tacy.

Betsy and Tacy had seen in Winona's face something that gave them a glimmer of hope. Inspired by the pokes, Tib looked and saw it too.

Winona was more interested in this play than she was in *Uncle Tom's Cabin*. After all, she went to plays at the Opera House often.

"Who's going to be Lady Clinton?" she repeated in an urgent voice.

Betsy looked at Tacy, and Tacy looked at Betsy.

"We haven't decided," said Tacy carelessly.

"We've got to be careful whom we pick," said Betsy. "It's a very important part. She's got to be dark. Lady Clinton is a whopping villainess, you know. And all villainesses are dark."

"She needs long black hair."

"And black eyes."

"And white teeth," said Tib, staring at Winona.

Winona laughed.

"Sounds sort of like me," she said, tossing her head.

"Oh, but it couldn't be you," said Betsy. "Because we're giving it Saturday afternoon."

"No, Betsy," broke in Tib.

"Why, yes we are," said Tacy, jabbing Tib violently. "Don't you remember?"

"Why do you have to give it Saturday?" asked Winona mistrustfully.

"Mrs. Muller wants us to give it before she housecleans downstairs. 'The sooner, the better,' she said. And we can get it up tomorrow if we hurry. I must get this finished, though." Betsy licked her pencil industriously. "The first scene is at Lord Patterson's ball."

At noon Betsy, Tacy, and Tib left the schoolhouse arm in arm. Winona joined them.

"Talking about your play?" she asked.

"Yes," said Betsy. "We're planning how we'll get Tib up to Heaven. If they get Little Eva up to Heaven at the Opera House, we ought to be able to do it with Tib in her back parlor. Do you know how they do it at the Opera House, Winona?"

"I can find out Saturday."

"That will be too late to do us any good," Betsy said regretfully.

"We could tie a rope to the gas chandelier," suggested Tacy. "When Tib dies, she could just shinny up."

"That doesn't seem very dignified," said Betsy.

"Besides," said Tib. "I don't think papa would like it. I might pull the chandelier down."

"She could climb up a ladder and sit there," Winona said. "You could decorate the ladder with pink tissue paper and make it look just like Heaven."

"That's a marvelous idea!" cried Betsy. "We could draw angels and cut them out and pin them to the ladder."

"And doves."

"And harps."

They looked at Winona with spontaneous admiration.

At recess that afternoon Betsy wrote on her play again.

"How's it coming?" asked Winona, prancing by.

"Gee whiz!" said Betsy. "The *trouble* this Lady Clinton has!"

"Going to get it done for tomorrow?"

51

"You bet!"

Betsy scribbled furiously.

After school Winona approached the three friends.

"Can't you come to my house to play?"

"I'm sorry," Betsy said. "We just can't. The play's done, and we've got to rehearse it. But I don't know *who* we'll get for Lady Clinton. In the ballroom scene she wears a velvet dress with a train and carries a peacock feather fan."

"I've got a peacock feather," Winona said. "And my mother's got a yellow velvet dress with a train. She'd let me wear it, I think."

"That would be peachy!"

"If you only could!"

There was an expectant pause.

"But do you suppose you'd know how to repent?" asked Betsy. "It's pretty hard. You have to carry on, I tell you."

She broke away from the rest, and clasped one hand to her forehead, the other to her heart beneath her sailor-suit pocket.

" 'Oh, my children!' " she cried in a deep vibrant voice. " 'Forgive me! Forgive me! I can ask you now for I am dying! I am on my death bed! My brow is damp! . . .' You'd have to weep real tears," said Betsy, resuming her normal tone.

Winona blinked.

"I could," she said. "You said yourself when we were playing statues that I was a regular actress."

"That's right," said Tacy.

"Well, it doesn't matter anyhow," said Betsy. "For you'll be busy tomorrow. You'll be at *Uncle Tom's Cabin.*"

Winona was thinking deeply.

"Can't that play possibly be postponed?" she asked.

"Why should it be?" Betsy replied. "We haven't anything else to do tomorrow."

"We'd sort of like to have something nice to do when *Uncle Tom's Cabin* is in town," Tacy admitted.

"Then we won't feel so bad about missing it," Tib said.

They could go no further.

They looked at Winona fixedly, in silence. There was a trapped look in her black eyes. But after a moment she grinned nonchalantly.

"Well, good-by," she said. She skipped jauntily away.

Betsy, Tacy, and Tib walked home on dragging feet. They did not even mention rehearsing for their play. All their interest in Lady Clinton, her sins and her repenting, had vanished.

At first it had been real. They had not planned to use their play as a device for attracting Winona. But her interest in it had raised ecstatic hopes which now were dashed to the ground.

They went to Tacy's house and sat by the pump again, but it was dreary there today. The weather was changing. Clouds dimmed the sky. A cold wind scurried the dead leaves.

Gyp ran up barking as though to ask merrily, "What about the play?" But they did not speak to him. They did not even throw a stick for him to retrieve.

"Come over to play after supper?" asked Betsy when the Big Mill whistles blew.

"I suppose so."

"I suppose we've got to rehearse."

"Sure."

But in their hearts they knew that they would not rehearse. They would not give their play. It was as dead as the leaves blowing down from the hill.

Tomorrow in the Opera House the great painted curtain would rise on the glories of *Uncle Tom's Cabin* . . . with them not there to see. Bloodhounds chasing Eliza, Topsy dancing, Little Eva dying and going to Heaven . . . and the three of them sitting at home. It was almost too much to bear.

"I wish we could of made her invite us," said Tib. Tears moistened her round blue eyes.

Betsy and Tacy did not look at each other. They were not accustomed to failure.

Julia came out on the front porch of the Ray house.

"Betsy," she called, sounding surprised. "Somebody wants to talk to you . . . over the telephone."

"The *telephone!*"

Betsy could hardly believe her ears. She was never called to the telephone. She had spoken over it, of course, talking to her father down at his shoe store to test the miracle. But she had never received a call before. No one she knew had a telephone.

At that point in her thoughts she remembered that someone she knew had a telephone, someone very important. Winona Root had a telephone.

As though her feet had sprouted wings, Betsy leaped up

the steps and into the house. Tacy and Tib flew after. She
ran to the telephone, jumped up on the stool and took the
dangling receiver into her hand.

"Hello."

"Hello. Is this you, Betsy? This is Winona Root."

"Hello, Winona."

"Hello. Can you hear me?"

"Yes, I can hear you."

"How are you?"

"Fine."

After a pause, Winona said: "You know those 'comps'

I've got for *Uncle Tom's Cabin?*"

"Yes."

"Four of them."

"Yes."

"Well, I want you and Tacy and Tib to go with me."

"Oh, do you?" Betsy said.

"Yes. I did all the time. I asked my father for four 'comps' just so's I could take you."

Betsy could not answer.

"We're going to sit in a box," Winona said.

Still Betsy was speechless with delight.

"Will you be at my house at twelve o'clock sharp?" Winona asked. "The matinee begins at two-thirty, and I like to get there early. I like to be out in front of the Opera House before the doors open, even."

Betsy felt a warmth of affectionate understanding, a warmth of fellowship. She had never been to a play before but she knew that she loved them just as Winona did.

"We'll be there," she said. "At your house. At twelve."

She put the receiver reverently into its hook.

V

UNCLE TOM'S CABIN

ND so Betsy, Tacy, and Tib went with Winona Root to see *Uncle Tom's Cabin.*

Instead of calling for Winona at noon, they called for her at half-past eleven. Since early morning all of them had been in a fever of impatience. They had started to get ready right after breakfast and had clamored for their dinners at ten o'clock. Their mothers were exhausted by the time the three girls, well scrubbed and wearing their Sunday best, rang the Root doorbell.

Winona was waiting, as impatient as themselves. Shortly after noon the expectant four stood under the canopy of the Opera House. While they waited for the doors to open, Winona entertained them by describing the inside of the building. Betsy, Tacy, and Tib hung on every word.

Outside, the Opera House was a large brick structure. It was a fine theatre for a town the size of Deep Valley. But Deep Valley was what is known as a good show town. It was a thriving county seat, and theatrical productions, passing from the Twin Cities to Omaha, found it a convenient and profitable one-night-stand.

Winona finished her eloquent description. Children by the dozens had joined them. She rehearsed the stories of all the plays she had seen; still the big doors did not open. Out of the jostling crowd two boys came into view, climbing one of the pillars that supported the canopy. The girls recognized Tom Slade and Herbert Humphreys. At the same moment, the boys saw them.

"So *that's* who you took," Herbert shouted to Winona, pointing at Betsy, Tacy, and Tib. He and Tom slid down the pillars and pushed their way through the crowd.

"You certainly were hard up for someone to take," said Tom.

"*We* wouldn't have gone with you, even if you'd asked us," said Herbert.

"Like fun you wouldn't," answered Winona, tossing her head.

Winona liked Herbert, just as Betsy, Tacy, and Tib did. He had attractions other than his knickerbockers. He was a handsome boy with thick blond hair, a rosy skin, and lively blue eyes. Tom was dark with shaggy hair. Ever since Herbert came to Deep Valley, the two had been friends.

"We're going to sit up in the peanut heaven and eat peanuts," said Tom.

"And throw the shells at people in the boxes."

"Spitballs too, at the people who have 'comps.' "

"Don't you dare!" Winona said.

They weren't quarreling. The boys thought it was fun to be talking to the girls. And the girls felt as old as Julia and Katie. They joked and laughed . . . except Tacy who blushed and didn't say much. Tacy wasn't bashful with Tom because she had known him all her life but she was bashful with the glorious Herbert Humphreys.

Herbert offered them peanuts and Tom pointed to a bill-board picture that showed Eliza running across the ice with the bloodhounds almost at her throat.

"I saw those dogs," he said. "A man had them out walking this morning. He let me pet them."

"*Pet* them!"

"Yes, but they're plenty wild, he says. He says Buffalo Bill would give a fortune for them. He's offered it, even, but the manager won't sell."

"Did you see Miss Evelyn Montmorency?"

"Who's she?"

"Just America's most talented and beautiful child actress, that's all."

"Is that so, smarty?"

"Who cares about her?" asked Herbert, hurling a peanut shell at the billboard where Little Eva was ascending into Heaven on the back of a milk-white dove.

There was a rattle at the big entrance doors. They swung open, showing Sunny Jim's smiling face. Children stampeded inside, toward the ticket window. Winona ignored the ticket window. With Betsy, Tacy, and Tib following her proudly, her 'comps' in her hand, she swaggered toward the inner door.

"Hello, Mr. Kendall."

"Hello, Winona."

Winona and Betsy and Tacy and Tib were the first ones inside the house.

They did not go at once to their box. First they raced all

over the auditorium. It was elegant beyond even Winona's descriptions and Betsy's wildest dreams. A giant chandelier hung with glittering crystal drops was suspended from the ceiling. The seats were upholstered in red velvet. The boxes were hung with red velvet tied back with golden cords.

"Isn't it beautiful?" Winona asked, enjoying their stupe-faction.

"Oh, Winona! It's wonderful! It's grand!"

"Didn't I tell you?" Winona acted as proud as though she and not Mr. Poppy had built it.

She raced up to the balcony, Betsy, Tacy, and Tib running after her. They all ran down the aisle and leaned over the railing. Tib leaned so far that Betsy and Tacy held on to her skirts.

Behind the balcony was the gallery where Tom and Herbert would sit.

"Those seats are the cheapest. Ten cents. This show is a ten, twent, thirt. The balcony costs twenty. The dress circle costs twenty, too, and the parquet, thirty."

Dress circle! Parquet! What were they?

They pelted back downstairs, and Winona pointed out the dress circle under the balcony. A low railing separated it from the parquet, down front. Where the dress circle met the parquet, in the very center of the house, were two wide, well-padded seats.

"Those are Mr. and Mrs. Poppy's seats. But they probably won't be here this afternoon. They'll come to the night show."

In this opinion Winona was mistaken. When she and her party reached their upper front box and, having explored its delights, seated themselves in the frail chairs overlooking the auditorium and stage, they saw Mrs. Poppy settling herself in one of the two spacious seats. She took out hatpins and lifted off a big plumed hat. Her hair shone like gold.

"There's Mrs. Poppy after all," Betsy cried. "For such a fat lady, Mrs. Poppy's pretty."

"Yes, she is. She's nice too," said Tib.

Leaning out of the box, with Betsy and Tacy holding her skirts again, Tib waved. Mrs. Poppy did not see her at first, but having been poked by children in adjoining seats, she looked up. Then her smile was as bright as the diamonds in her ears. She waved happily back.

There was a great deal of waving, calling, and whistling going on. Tom and Herbert whistled through their fingers and threw peanut shells as they had promised until the girls in the box stopped turning around.

Betsy stopped turning around because somewhere down in the bowels of the Opera House violins were being tuned. She sat back rapturously and read her program through. Then she gave her attention to the curtain on which a gentleman in a sedan chair and beautiful ladies in hoop skirts were transfixed in a gay romantic moment. There was a flower booth behind them. There were some hens scratching at the front.

A workman came out and crossed the stage. The audience clapped vociferously. Men filed into the orchestra pit. The children clapped some more. The boys in the gallery whistled and gave cat calls. Mrs. Poppy looked up at the box and put her hands over her ears for a joke. Winona, Betsy, Tacy, and Tib clapped harder than ever, laughing down at Mrs. Poppy.

The orchestra started to play. It played sad tunes. *Old Kentucky Home. Swanee River, Massa's in de Cold Cold Ground.* All over the house the lights went low. There were rainbow colors in the crystals of the great chandelier as the lights faded away. Then . . . oh, magic moment! . . . the curtain started to rise. Slowly, slowly, while the music kept on playing and the rainbow in the chandelier flickered out, forgotten, the curtain lifted. Betsy reached out for Tacy's hand and squeezed it. She wanted to share this rapturous moment of the curtain going up.

Sympathetically Tacy squeezed back. By now the full stage was revealed. They saw a Negro cabin. The slave Eliza sitting with her child . . .

Betsy and Tacy still clasped hands but they forgot each other and everything but the play.

The story unfolded in dramatic scenes which kept the four girls in a front upper box rigid with excitement. George, Eliza's husband, ran away. Eliza, hearing that her child was to be sold, ran away too. She reached the icy river.

"Better sink beneath its cold waters with my child locked in my arms than have him torn from me and sold into bondage!"

The ferocious pack of man-eating Siberian bloodhounds leaped into view. (There were two in the pack.) Eliza took to the ice.

"Courage, my child! We will be free . . . or perish!"

Miraculously she escaped, and the party in the box relaxed, but only for a moment.

Presently they were in the elegant St. Clare parlor. The languid Marie lay on the couch. Little Eva ran in, her yellow curls flowing about her.

"Mamma!" she cried in a sweet piping voice.

"Take care! Don't make my head ache."

St. Clare came in, and good old Uncle Tom, and funny Aunt Ophelia with her corkscrew curls, and the comical Topsy.

The audience laughed uproariously at Topsy.

"I 'spect I growed," she said. "Don't think nobody never made me."

She sang a song about it.

> "Oh, white folks I was neber born,
> Aunt Sue, she raised me in de corn . . ."

She danced her breakdown, and Tib poked Betsy.

"I could do that," she said.

The waits between the acts of the play did not break the spell. A black-faced quartette sang plantation melodies, told jokes, and cakewalked. The girls did not talk very much. They waited for that moment of unfailing rapture when the curtain would go up.

Little Eva hung garlands of flowers around the neck of Uncle Tom. She told him she was going to die.

"They come to me in my sleep, those spirits bright. Uncle Tom, I'm going there."

"Where, Miss Eva?"

"I'm going *there*, to the spirits bright. Tom, I'm going before long."

And in the next scene she expired, breathing, "O love, O joy, O peace." Sad music played, and she was glimpsed in Heaven.

Tacy's weeping almost shook the box. Betsy joined her tears to Tacy's, and Tib put her head into Betsy's lap to cry. Even Winona cried, big brilliant tears that glittered in her eyes after the curtain went down.

But there was worse to come.

St. Clare died without signing the freedom papers for Uncle Tom. Uncle Tom was sold down the river. He was flogged by Simon Legree. Tacy kept her eyes shut tight, but that could not keep out the dreadful crack of the lash.

At the end the scene showed sunset clouds. Little Eva, robed in white, sat upon a milk-white dove. Her hands were extended over St. Clare, her father, and Uncle Tom, kneeling below. The music was stately. The curtain went slowly down.

There was an uproar of applause and the curtain went up and down again, not once but many times. All the actors came out to bow, even those who had died in the play, which was very consoling.

Uncle Tom came, and Tacy wiped her eyes and sniffed. St. Clare came, looking very handsome. And his wife, Marie, not lazy and complaining now, but smiling and happy.

Aunt Ophelia came. And Topsy. And Simon Legree. When Simon Legree appeared the boys in the gallery hissed and booed, and Simon Legree laughed, and cracked his big whip.

Little Eva, of course, came again and again, still wearing her heavenly robes, her yellow curls shining. She came with the entire cast, and she came with Uncle Tom, and with her father, and mother, and Topsy. She bowed to them and to the audience and smiled and kissed her hands.

Betsy, Tacy, Tib, and Winona clapped and cheered and pounded. At last the curtain came down to stay down. The play was over.

"Didn't I tell you it was good?" Winona asked. She seemed to feel that she had written the play and acted every part.

Betsy didn't mind. She felt warm inside toward Winona. Winona had given her this wonderful gift of the play. And Winona loved it just as she did.

Reluctantly they put on their hats and jackets. Even as they had been the first to enter, they were the last to leave the Opera House. Everyone knew Winona . . . the ushers, the cleaning women. They greeted her cordially and she greeted them. Betsy, Tacy, and Tib were awed and proud.

"If you like," said Winona grandly as they went through the big front doors, "we can go around in back and see Little Eva come out."

"Winona! Can we really?"

Betsy, Tacy, and Tib were almost overwhelmed with the magnificence of this idea.

"Of course. I do it often," Winona said nonchalantly.

She led them around the side of the Opera House. A small crowd of children had preceded them. Herbert and Tom were there, but now they did not joke with the girls. Their eyes were burning; their talk was all of the show.

"Gosh darn, those bloodhounds were fierce!"

"And to think I *touched* them today!"

"Did you see their jaws drip?"

"Golly, yes! Do you think they'll come out, Winona?"

"I don't think so. You see, there's a show tonight. They'll probably be fed inside."

They all stared expectantly at the stage door that said in big white letters, "Private. Keep out."

It swung open and a man in a silk hat emerged. Swinging a cane, he walked briskly down the alley.

"Was that St. Clare?"

"Naw! Too old."

"It was too St. Clare. I recognized him."

The door swung open again, and again. More silk toppers, canes, and fancy vests with watch chains draped across them. Large dashing hats, short pleated jackets, sweeping skirts,

pocket books dangling from chains. Men and women looking remotely like the characters in the play came out by ones
and twos. Some looked tired; others were fresh and gay;
many showed traces of burned cork.

"Is that Uncle Tom?" "Is that Topsy?" "There comes
Simon Legree!"

Most of the stage folk smiled when they heard the whis-
pers. Simon Legree cracked an imaginary whip.

At last a woman came out with a little girl, unmistakably
Little Eva. The rosy cheeks she had had in the play were
gone; she was pale. But the shining light curls were the same.
Her bonnet and coat were of blue velveteen. She wore white
kid gloves and carried a small purse on a chain.

She and the woman (who looked ever so faintly like
Eliza), walked up the alley and over to Front Street. Betsy

and Tacy, Tib, and Winona followed at a respectful distance behind. Tom and Herbert followed too, still burning-eyed. Now and then the little girl turned around. Her eyes were large and blue.

To the surprise of all, the woman did not stop at the fine big Melborn Hotel. She and Little Eva proceeded up Front Street to the Deep Valley House. This was the place farmers stayed when they came to town. There was a hitching shed for horses behind the low wooden structure.

"If I was Evelyn Montmorency," said Tib, "I'd stay at the Melborn Hotel."

It was just like Tib to mention that. Betsy and Tacy and Winona all spoke quickly.

"She could stay there if she wanted to."

"I should say she could! The most beautiful and talented child actress in America!"

"Probably it just didn't pay them. They're leaving town so soon."

At the door of the Deep Valley House, the little girl turned around again. She smiled at the children, not radiantly as she had smiled on the stage, but shyly.

"Good-by," she said.

"Good-by," shouted Betsy, Tacy, Tib, and Winona.

"Good-by," said Herbert and Tom.

Unexpectedly, they pulled off their caps, staring in adoration.

Little Eva went into the Deep Valley House and the door closed behind her. The children did not see her again. But none of them was ever to forget her.

VI

BETSY'S DESK

ETSY, Tacy, and Tib did not give "*The Repentance of Lady Clinton.*" Winona understood. She understood so well that she never even mentioned it. They gave plenty of plays that year, and Winona was in them, but they did not give that one.

Mrs. Muller cleaned her downstairs without the satisfaction of having it mussed up first. Uncle Keith's costumes were aired and put away without having had their hour on the boards. Betsy helped her mother fold the garments and lay them in the flat-topped trunk. As they worked she asked questions, for since seeing *Uncle Tom's Cabin* she had a new interest in her actor-uncle.

"He'll come home sometime," Mrs. Ray said. "He must want to see me again, just as I want to see him. He was awfully hurt and angry when he left. And he doesn't know that our stepfather has gone out to California with mother."

"Do you think he's still an actor, mamma?"

"Yes, I do. Of course he went into the Spanish War. But if anything had happened to him the government would have told us. He must be just trouping, waiting for the big success he wanted to have before he came home.

" 'I'll come home, Jule, when I have a feather in my cap.'

That's what he said when he said good-by to me." Betsy's mother paused in folding a Roman toga, and her face grew sad with the old sad memory of the night Keith ran away.

"What did he look like, mamma?" asked Betsy, although she had heard a hundred times.

"He looked like me," Mrs. Ray answered. "That is, he was tall and thin with a pompadour of red wavy hair. His eyes were brighter than mine, so full of fun and mischief. And he had the gayest smile I ever saw. None of you children look like him. You look like your father and his sisters. You get plenty of talents from your Uncle Keith, though."

Mrs. Ray's voice lifted proudly. She finished folding the Roman toga and laid it into the trunk.

"Does Julia get her reciting from him?" asked Betsy, knowing the answer well.

"Yes, she does. And her beautiful singing voice. And her gift at the piano. How Keith could make the piano keys fly, though he never had a lesson in his life! He could play and sing as well as act and he could draw and paint and model and write . . ."

"Write!" cried Betsy. She always loved to hear about the writing part.

"Yes, write. He wrote poems, plays, stories, everything. He was always scribbling, just as you are. And that reminds me, Betsy. Isn't it getting pretty cold to write up in the maple tree?"

Mrs. Ray knew all about the office in the maple tree. She had given Betsy the cigar box. Betsy's mother was a great believer in people having private places.

"Yes, it is," said Betsy. "I haven't been writing lately."

"You must bring your papers indoors then. Your father and I are very proud of your writing. We want you to keep at it. You ought to have a desk but we can't afford one yet. I'll find a place for your things, though."

Mrs. Ray smoothed the last costume into place and closed the trunk.

"Rena will help me lift this into the garret," she said. "Come on into your room, Betsy."

Betsy followed her mother into the front bedroom. It was a small room with low tentlike walls. There was a single window at the front looking across to Tacy's house and the trees and the sunsets behind it. The big bed for Julia and Betsy, the small bed for Margaret, the chest of drawers, and the commode for wash bowl and pitcher filled the room.

Mrs. Ray pulled out the drawers in the chest. They were all crammed full. She looked around in some perplexity.

"I could make a place for your things in the back parlor," she said. "But I've noticed that you like to get away by yourself when you write."

"Yes, I do," said Betsy.

"It's got to be here then," Mrs. Ray answered. She tapped her lips thoughtfully.

"I have it!" she cried after a moment, her eyes flashing as brightly as she had said that Uncle Keith's used to flash.

"What?" asked Betsy.

"The trunk. Uncle Keith's trunk. You may have that for a desk. It can fit here under the window out of the way. It's just the thing."

She ran back into Rena's room and Betsy followed. They opened the trunk again. Swiftly her mother stowed the articles filling the tray into the bottom compartment.

"You can have the tray for your papers," she told Betsy happily. "Just wait until I get it fixed up!"

Mrs. Ray loved to fix things up around her house. And when she got started, Mr. Ray often said, she didn't let any grass grow under her feet.

She called down the stairs to Rena.

"Will you come up, please? Bring some shelf paper with scalloped edging. And my old brown shawl. And a couple of pillows."

"What are the shawl and pillows for?" asked Betsy, dancing about with excitement.

"They're to make a little window seat out of the trunk when you're not writing. When you feel like writing, you'll put the pillows on the floor and sit on them and open your desk. It's much nicer than an ordinary desk, because it's a real theatrical trunk."

Betsy thought so too.

Rena came up the stairs on a run. She was used to Mrs. Ray's lightning ideas. They carried the trunk into the front bedroom and placed it beneath the window. Mrs. Ray started papering the tray.

"I'll go out to get my things," said Betsy joyfully.

She ran down the stairs and out the door and waded through golden leaves to the back-yard maple.

When she reached the crotch where the cigar box was nailed, she looked out on a scene rivaling Little Eva's

Heaven. The maples of Hill Street were golden clouds; and the encircling hillside made a backdrop of more clouds, copper colored, wine-red and crimson. The sky was brightly blue.

It was a sight to make one catch one's breath, but there was a chill in the air. Betsy brushed the dead leaves off the cigar box and opened it. A squirrel had already entered claim to possession. Six butternuts were there.

Hurriedly Betsy gathered up her belongings. Those tablets marked "Ray's Shoe Store. Wear Queen Quality Shoes," in which her novels were written. Two stubby pencils. An eraser. Some odds and ends of paper on which she had made verses. Leaving the Spanish lady to guard the butternuts, she wriggled down the tree.

She rushed eagerly into the kitchen and started up the stairs two at a time. Halfway up, she slowed her pace a little. It occurred to her to wonder whether her mother would notice the titles of her books.

Her mother did not read Betsy's writing without express permission. And she did not allow anyone else to do so. She was very particular about it. But these titles were printed out so big and bold. She could hardly help seeing them. And if she did, she would know that Betsy had been reading Rena's novels.

Betsy walked slowly with a suddenly flushed face into the front bedroom.

"It's all ready," her mother called cheerfully. Rena, Betsy saw, was gone. "I've finished papering it. Doesn't it look pretty?"

It did.

"Here is a case for your pencils. I'll ask papa to bring you fresh ones, and an eraser, and a little ten-cent dictionary. Perhaps you would like to put in a book or two? The Bible and Longfellow?"

"Yes, I would," said Betsy. Her mother noticed her changed voice. She looked up quickly and saw that Betsy was hugging her tablets secretively to her breast.

"You can put the tablets right into this corner," Mrs. Ray said. "Don't think I might ask to read them, dear. I won't. Keith was just like you about that. He never wanted anyone to read what he was writing until he was through with it, and sometimes not then. Whenever you show anything you've written to papa or me, we're interested and proud. But never feel that you have to."

Betsy threw the tablets roughly into the trunk.

"I don't care if you read them."

"But I don't want to read them," said her mother, looking troubled, "unless you want me to. The whole idea of this desk is to give you privacy. There is even a key to it, you know."

"Read them," said Betsy crossly. She turned away and scowled.

Mrs. Ray gathered up the tablets. The titles flashed past. *Lady Gwendolyn's Sin. The Tall Dark Stranger. Hardly More than a Child.*

For quite a while she did not say a word. She did not open the books. She just stacked them into a pile which she shaped with her hands, thoughtfully.

Betsy stole a glance at her mother's profile, fine and straight like George Washington's. It did not look angry, but it looked serious, grave.

"I think," said Mrs. Ray at last, "that Rena must have been sharing her dime novels with you."

Betsy did not answer.

"Betsy, it's a mistake for you to read that stuff. There's no great harm in it, but if you're going to be a writer you need to read good books. They train you to write, build up your mind. We have good books in the bookcase downstairs. Why don't you read them?"

"I've read them all," said Betsy.

"Of course," said her mother. "I never thought of that."

She took her hands away from the neat pile. The tray of the trunk, with its lining of scalloped blue paper looked fresh and inviting. Betsy felt ashamed.

"I'll throw those stories away if you want me to," she said.

"No," answered her mother. "Not until *you* want to." She still looked thoughtful. Then her face lighted up as it had when she thought of using Uncle Keith's trunk for a desk.

"I have a plan," she said. "A splendid plan. But I have to talk it over with papa."

"When will I know about it?"

"Tonight, maybe. Yes, I think you will know tonight before you go to bed."

Smiling, Mrs. Ray jumped up and closed the trunk. She and Betsy arranged the brown shawl and the pillows.

"It's almost like a cozy-corner," Mrs. Ray said.

She and Betsy ran downstairs and told Julia and Margaret about the new desk. Betsy ran outdoors to find Tacy and Tib and tell them. She brought them in to see it, and they liked it very much.

She kept wondering what the plan was. And after supper she found out. She had been playing games out in the street with the neighborhood children. Julia and Katie didn't play out any more. They were too grown up or too busy or had too many lessons or something. Margaret and the Rivers children played, and Paul and Freddie and Hobbie, and somehow the street seemed to belong to them even more than it did to Betsy, Tacy, and Tib.

When Margaret and Betsy went into the house, Julia was writing to Jerry. Their father and mother were reading beside the back-parlor lamp. Their father was reading a newspaper and their mother was reading a novel. It wasn't a paper-backed novel like Rena's. It was called *When Knighthood Was in Flower*.

Margaret climbed up on her father's lap and he put down his newspaper. Mrs. Ray put down her novel. She smiled at her husband.

"Papa has that plan all worked out," she said. "Tell her about it, Bob."

Mr. Ray crossed his legs, hoisted Margaret to a comfortable position and began.

"Well, Betsy," he said, "your mother tells me that you are going to use Uncle Keith's trunk for a desk. That's fine. You need a desk. I've often noticed how much you like to write. The way you eat up those advertising tablets from the store! I never saw anything like it. I can't understand it though. I never write anything but checks myself."

"Bob!" said Mrs. Ray. "You wrote the most wonderful letters to me before we were married. I still have them, a big bundle of them. Every time I clean house I read them over and cry."

"Cry, eh?" said Mr. Ray, grinning. "In spite of what your mother says, Betsy, if you have any talent for writing, it comes from her family. Her brother Keith was mighty talented, and maybe you are too. Maybe you're going to be a writer."

Betsy was silent, agreeably abashed.

"But if you're going to be a writer," he went on, "you've got to read. Good books. Great books. The classics. And fortunately . . . that's what I'm driving at . . . Deep Valley has a new Carnegie Library, almost ready to open. White marble building, sunny, spick and span, just full of books."

"I know," Betsy said.

"That library," her father continued, "is going to be just what you need. And your mother and I want you to get acquainted with it. Of course it's way down town, but you're old enough now to go down town alone. Julia goes down to her music lessons, since the Williamses moved away, and this is just as important."

He shifted his position, and his hand went into his pocket.

"As I understand it," he said, "you can keep a book two weeks. So, after the library opens, why don't you start going down . . . every other Saturday, say . . . and get some books? And don't hurry home. Stay a while. Browse around among the books. Every time you go, you can take fifteen cents." He gave her two coins. "At noon go over to Bier-bauer's Bakery for a sandwich and milk and ice cream. Would you like that?"

"Oh, papa!" said Betsy. She could hardly speak.

She thought of the library, so shining white and new; the rows and rows of unread books; the bliss of unhurried sojourns there and of going out to a restaurant, alone, to eat.

"I'd like it," she said in a choked voice. "I'd like it a lot."

Julia was as happy as Betsy was, almost. One nice thing about Julia was that she rejoiced in other people's luck.

78

"It's a wonderful plan, papa," she cried. "I've thought for ages that Betsy was going to be a writer."

"I thought Betsy learned to write a long time ago," said Margaret, staring out of her new English bob.

Everyone laughed, and Mrs. Ray explained to Margaret what kind of writer Betsy might come to be.

Betsy was so full of joy that she had to be alone. She ran upstairs to her bedroom and sat down on Uncle Keith's trunk. Behind Tacy's house the sun had set. A wind had sprung up and the trees, their color dimmed, moved under a brooding sky. All the stories she had told Tacy and Tib seemed to be dancing in those trees, along with all the stories

she planned to write some day and all the stories she would read at the library. Good stories. Great stories. The classics. Not like Rena's novels.

She pulled off the pillows and shawl and opened her desk. She took out the pile of little tablets and ran with them down to the kitchen and lifted the lid of the stove and shoved them in. Then she walked into the back parlor, dusting off her hands.

"Papa," she said, "will you bring me some more tablets? Quite a lot of them, please."

VII

A TRIP TO THE LIBRARY

ARLY in November Betsy made her first expedition to the library.

It was a windy day. Gray clouds like battleships moved across a purplish sea of sky. It looked like snow, Mrs. Ray remarked as she and Julia stood on the front porch seeing Betsy off. She looked a little doubtfully at Betsy's Sunday hat, a flowered brim that left her ears perilously exposed.

"Oughtn't you to wear your hood, Betsy?"

"Mamma! Not when I'm going down town to the new Carnegie Library!"

"You'd better put on leggins and overshoes though."

"There isn't a speck of snow on the ground."

Mrs. Ray looked at the thick woolen stockings, the stout high shoes.

"All right. Just button your coat. But if it snows, walk over to the store and ride home with papa."

"I will," Betsy promised.

She tried to act as though it were nothing to go to the library alone. But her happiness betrayed her. Her smile could not be restrained, and it spread from her tightly pressed mouth, to her round cheeks, almost to the hair ribbons tied in perky bows over her ears.

Julia had loaned her a pocket book to hold her fifteen cents. It dangled elegantly from a chain over Betsy's mittened hand. Betsy opened it and looked inside to see that her money was safe. She closed it again and took the chain firmly into her grasp.

"Good-by," she said, kissing her mother and Julia.

"Good-by," she waved to Rena, who was smiling through the window.

"Good-by," she called to Margaret, who was playing on the hill as the small girls of Hill Street did on a Saturday morning. Betsy could remember well when she used to do it herself. (It was only last Saturday.)

Tacy ran across the street to walk to the corner with her. It was a little hard, parting from Tacy. They were so used to doing everything together.

"I wish you were coming too," Betsy said.

"I'll be all right. I'm going to play with Tib."

"Some Saturday soon you'll be coming."

"Sure I will."

In spite of her brave words Tacy sounded forlorn. She looked forlorn, bareheaded, the wind pulling her curls.

But at the corner she hugged Betsy's arm. She looked into Betsy's eyes with her deep blue eyes that were always so loving and kind.

"I *want* you to go," she said. "Why, I've always known you were going to be a writer. I knew it ahead of everyone."

Betsy felt all right about going then. She kissed Tacy and went off at a run.

The big elm in Lincoln Park, bare and austere, pointed

the way down town. She entered Broad Street, passing big houses cloaked in withered vines against November cold. She passed the corner where she usually turned off to go to her father's store and kept briskly on until she reached the library.

This small white marble temple was glittering with newness. Betsy went up the immaculate steps, pulled open the shining door.

She entered a bit self-consciously, never having been in a library before. She saw an open space with a big cage in the center, a cage such as they had in the bank, with windows in it. Behind rose an orderly forest of bookcases, tall and dark, with aisles between.

Betsy advanced to the cage and the young lady sitting inside smiled at her. She had a cozy little face, with half a dozen tiny moles. Her eyes were black and dancing. Her hair was black too, curly and untidy.

"Are you looking for the Children's Room?" she asked.

Betsy beamed in response.

"Well, not exactly. That is, I'd like to see it. But I may not want to read just in the Children's Room."

"You don't think so?" asked the young lady, sounding surprised.

"No. You see," explained Betsy, "I want to read the classics."

"You do?"

"Yes. All of them. I hope I'm going to like them."

The young lady looked at her with a bright intensity. She got down off her stool.

"I know a few you'll like," she said. "And they happen to be in the Children's Room. Come on. I'll show you."

The Children's Room was exactly right for children. The tables and chairs were low. Low bookshelves lined the walls, and tempting-looking books with plenty of illustrations were open on the tables. There was a big fireplace in the room, with a fire throwing up flames and making crackling noises. Above it was the painting of a rocky island with a temple on it, called *The Isle of Delos.*

"That's one of the Greek islands," said Miss Sparrow. Miss Sparrow was the young lady's name; she had told Betsy so. "There's nothing more classic than Greece," she said. "Do you know Greek mythology? No? Then let's begin on that."

She went to the shelves and returned with a book.

"*Tanglewood Tales*, by Nathaniel Hawthorne. Mythology. Classic," she said.

She went back to the shelves and returned with an armful of books. She handed them to Betsy one by one.

"*Tales from Shakespeare*, by Charles and Mary Lamb. Classic. *Don Quixote*, by Miguel de Cervantes. Classic. *Gulliver's Travels*, by Jonathan Swift. Classic. *Tom Sawyer*, by Mark Twain. Classic, going-to-be."

She was laughing, and so was Betsy.

"You don't need to read them all today," Miss Sparrow said.

"May I get a card and take some home?"

"You may have a card, but you'll have to get it signed before you draw out books. You may stay here and read though, as long as you like."

"Thank you," Betsy said.

Miss Sparrow went away.

Betsy took off her hat and coat. She was the only child in the room. Others came in shortly, but now she was all alone.

She seated herself in the chair nearest the fire, piled the books beside her and opened *Tanglewood Tales*. But she did not start to read at once. Before she began she smiled at the fire, she smiled at her books, she smiled broadly all around the room.

When the Big Mill whistle blew for twelve o'clock, she was surprised. She got up and put on her things.

"Did you have a good time?" Miss Sparrow asked, as Betsy passed the desk.

"Yes. I did."

"Be sure to come again."

"Oh," said Betsy, "I'll be back just as soon as I eat."

"But I thought you lived way up on Hill Street?"

"I do. But I'm eating at Bierbauer's Bakery. My father gave me fifteen cents. I'm going to eat there every time I come to the library," Betsy explained. "It's so I can take my time here, browse around among the books."

Miss Sparrow regarded her with the brightly intent look that Betsy had observed before.

"What a beautiful plan!" Miss Sparrow said.

Eating at Bierbauer's Bakery was almost as much fun as reading before the fire. It was warm in the bakery, and there was a delicious smell. Betsy bought a bologna sandwich, made of thick slices of freshly baked bread. She had a glass of milk too, and ice cream for dessert. But she decided that she wouldn't always have ice cream for dessert. Sometimes she would have jelly roll. It looked so good inside the glass counter.

Betsy couldn't help wondering if the other people in the bakery weren't surprised to see a girl her age eating there all alone. Whenever anyone looked at her she smiled. She was smiling most of the time.

On the way back to the library she looked eagerly for snow. She hoped she would have to call for her father. She loved visiting the store, riding the movable ladders from which he took boxes from the highest shelves, helping herself to the advertising tablets, talking to customers. But there wasn't a flake in the air. The battleships had changed to feather beds, hanging dark and low in the purplish sky.

Betsy returned to her chair, took off her coat and hat, opened her book and forgot the world again.

She looked up suddenly from *The Miraculous Pitcher* to see flakes coming past the window. They were coming thick and fast. She ran to look outdoors and saw that they had been coming for some time. Roofs and branches and the once brown lawns were already drenched in white.

"Now I've got to go to the store," she thought with satisfaction. She hurried into her wraps, said good-by to Miss Sparrow.

"It's too bad," said Miss Sparrow, "to take that pretty hat out into the snow."

"I haven't far to go," said Betsy. "I'm going to the store to ride home with my father. I'll see you in two weeks."

"Good-by," Miss Sparrow said.

Betsy's shoes made black tracks on the sidewalk. But the snow covered them at once. Filmy flakes settled on her coat and mittens. Soon she was cloaked in white. The air was filled with flakes, coming ever thicker and faster. Betsy ran and slid and slid again. She longed for Tacy and Tib. It was the first snow of the winter and demanded company.

She was soon to have it.

At the Opera House she paused to stare up at the posters. She wondered if there were a matinee coming. Winona would take them if there were. Then she noticed Mr. Poppy's horseless carriage, standing in front of the livery stable, blanketed in snow. She had not seen it since the day Tib took her ride, and she ran to inspect it.

A soft ball hit the back of her head. She whirled around. It was the worst thing she could have done. A snowball broke in her face.

She stooped blindly to mold a ball herself.

"All dressed up in her Sunday hat," somebody yelled.

A volley hit her hat, knocking it off. Snow oozed down the collar of her coat.

Her assailants were boys she had never seen before. She was one to three or four, and never any good at snowballs. Besides, she was handicapped by holding Julia's pocket book. She grabbed her hat and started to run.

She slipped on the soft snow. Swish! her feet went up!

Bang! she clattered down.

Yelling fiendishly, the boys ran away.

A little man came out of the livery stable and helped her to her feet. Behind him came a very large lady whose fur coat breathed a sweet perfume. Sunny Jim and Mrs. Poppy helped Betsy to her feet.

"Did you hurt yourself?" asked Mrs. Poppy.

"No ma'am. Not a bit." Betsy winked back the tears of which she was ashamed.

"They were bad boys."

"If I knew who they were," said Betsy, shaking off snow, "I'd bring Tacy and Tib and come back. Tib would fix them. She can throw snowballs better than any boy."

"Tib?" asked Mrs. Poppy. "My little friend Tib?"

"That's right. We waved to you from the box at *Uncle Tom's Cabin*. Tib and Tacy and Winona and me."

"Of course. I know you. But I don't know your name."

"Betsy Ray."

"Her pa runs Ray's Shoe Store," said Sunny Jim. "I know him well."

"I'm on my way to the shoe store now," said Betsy. "To ride home with my father." She shook the snow from her hat and put it on her head, grasped Julia's pocket book firmly. "Thank you for helping me," she said.

Mrs. Poppy was looking down at Betsy's feet.

"Speaking of shoes," she said, "yours are very wet, and your stockings are sopping. Why don't you come over to the hotel and dry out? I can telephone your father."

"Why . . . why . . . I'd love to," said Betsy.

"We'll have some hot chocolate with whipped cream," said Mrs. Poppy. She spoke fast and eagerly, like a child planning a party.

Her face alight, she turned to Sunny Jim.

"Just tell Mr. Poppy I won't wait. Tell him I've gone on home. It's just a step."

"Yes, Mrs. Poppy," said Sunny Jim respectfully.

Mrs. Poppy took Betsy's hand. They started toward Front Street through waving curtains of snow. The visit to the Carnegie Library raced into Betsy's past before a future which held hot chocolate at the Melborn Hotel.

VIII

MRS. POPPY

WHAT an adventure to tell Tacy and Tib! thought Betsy, as she waited for Mrs. Poppy in the big lobby that smelled of cigars and of the fat red leather chairs.

Winona too would have to hear about it. Winona had been in the Melborn Hotel, of course. But Betsy doubted that she had ever had hot chocolate in Mrs. Poppy's rooms; she doubted that Winona had ever come in as she had, hurrying gaily through the swinging door with Mrs. Poppy herself.

Mrs. Poppy was large and elegant in her black sealskin coat. Beneath the matching cap shone her yellow hair and the diamonds in her ears. Her face too shone with pleasure as she came back from the telephone behind the big desk.

"Your father says you may stay. I'm going to take you to the store at five o'clock. There's time for a real party," Mrs. Poppy exclaimed.

She held Betsy's hand and looked around the lobby.

"Which would you rather do?" she asked. "Take the elevator, or walk up the stairs?"

Betsy hesitated. She had never ridden in an elevator. But she looked at the grand staircase rising at the end of the lobby. It was richly carpeted, and there was a statue on the landing.

"The stairs," she said. "And the elevator coming down."

They climbed slowly. The sealskin coat was soft and cold when Betsy brushed against it. It smelled sweetly of Mrs. Poppy, and her silken skirts swished in Betsy's ears.

Betsy looked around often to get a view of the lobby which stretched impressively to the large plate glass windows, veiled now by snowflakes.

The statue on the landing had no head. It was the statue of a woman, or an angel . . .

"It's called the *Winged Victory*. It's Greek," said Mrs. Poppy.

"Greek!" said Betsy. "It's probably a goddess then." She walked around it, staring. Her reading of the day illumined the triumphant figure.

At the top of the stairs stretched the hotel dining room. It was two stories high and overlooked the river. Here Deep Valley gave its fashionable parties, its dances and cotillions, with an orchestra playing behind potted palms and those guests who did not care to dance amusing themselves with whist and euchre in the luxurious parlors. Betsy had read all about it many times in the society columns of Winona's father's paper.

She looked about her eagerly as Mrs. Poppy paused to speak to a maid in a white cap.

"Will you send in some hot chocolate?" she asked. "Plenty of whipped cream, please, and a plate of cakes."

"Yes, Mrs. Poppy," answered the maid, smiling at Betsy.

Mrs. Poppy tripped down a corridor, carpeted so deeply that their footfalls could not be heard. At the end she paused, took a key out of her bag and opened a door. They were greeted by a burst of warmth and of Mrs. Poppy's perfume.

"This is my little house," she said, leading the way inside.

It was indeed like a little house, a doll's house. (But Mrs. Poppy was a pretty big doll.) There were parlor, den, bedroom and bath; no dining room or kitchen.

"We eat in the big dining room, or else have our meals sent in here," Mrs. Poppy explained.

They went first into the bedroom which was blue, blue,

blue. Blue flowers climbed up the walls and blue flowers bloomed on the carpet. Blue draped the windows, the bed, the bureau and the chiffonier. The bathroom where Mrs. Poppy asked Betsy to take off her shoes and stockings was blue too.

Mrs. Poppy brought out a pair of bedroom slippers lined with white fur. Into these Betsy thrust her feet, while Mrs. Poppy took off her own wraps. Her dress was very modish with braid appliquéd on the blousy waist, the baggy sleeves, the trailing skirts. There was a fresh white bow at her neck.

Although she was so large, Mrs. Poppy looked young after her hat was removed. Her blonde hair was dressed in a high pompadour with a figure eight down her neck. Her skin was freshly pink, and her dark-lashed blue eyes brimmed with smiles.

Beside the bed was a small rocking chair with a doll in it.

"Was this your doll when you were a little girl?" Betsy asked.

"No," said Mrs. Poppy. "That doll belonged to our little girl, our Minnie. She died, and that's why I like to borrow other people's little girls sometimes."

"Oh," said Betsy. She was sorry. She wished she knew how to say she was sorry; Julia would have known. But Mrs. Poppy seemed to understand. She took Betsy's hand and squeezed it.

"Come on," she said. "Let me show you my little house."

They swished through leather portieres into the den. It was almost filled by a sofa piled with burned-leather pillows. The walls were crowded with Gibson Girls and Remington cowboys. There was a plate-rack full of beer steins, and on a table beside a capacious Morris chair was Mr. Poppy's collection of pipes.

"When Mr. Poppy is in here, there isn't room for me," Mrs. Poppy said laughing.

They swished through bead portieres into the parlor. Pink ribbons tied back long lace curtains that fell to the mossily carpeted floor. More pink ribbons were woven through wicker chairs and tables. A full-length mirror, framed in gold, stood between the windows reflecting the pictures on the walls, the great horn of a graphophone and a piano covered with velvet drapery and loaded with photographs.

While Mrs. Poppy opened a table underneath one of the windows and spread it with a white embroidered cloth, Betsy sat on the piano stool and looked at the music. There were popular songs . . . *Hiawatha, Bluebell;* there were the books of musical comedies . . . *The Prince of Pilsen, The Silver Slipper, The Belle of New York;* there were albums of piano pieces and the same Czerny that Julia was forever practicing.

"Do you play the piano?" asked Mrs. Poppy as she put cups and saucers, hand painted with roses, out on the table.

"No. But my sister Julia does. She plays and sings and speaks pieces and everything. You ought to hear her speak 'Editha's Burglar,'" Betsy said. She often bragged about Julia when Julia wasn't around.

"Have you any other brothers and sisters?"

"Yes. A little sister, Margaret. She has an English bob. She's cute, and not so much trouble as she used to be. She goes to school now."

"Tell me about your friends Tacy and Tib," said Mrs. Poppy, laying out spoons.

Betsy told her gladly. She told her how long the three of them had been friends, and about the good times they had together. She told her how Winona had taken them to see *Uncle Tom's Cabin* and how they had liked it and how they had followed Little Eva to the Deep Valley House.

Betsy liked to talk. Her father always said she got it from her mother, and her mother always said she got it from her father. But whomever she got it from she was certainly a talker. Sitting on the piano stool, swung about to face a smiling Mrs. Poppy, Betsy talked so fast and hard that they were both surprised when the maid knocked at the door.

"There's our chocolate already," Mrs. Poppy said.

The maid brought in the pot of chocolate, a bowl of whipped cream, and a plate of cakes. Betsy and Mrs. Poppy sat down at the little table by the window. It had stopped snowing now.

Like the hotel dining room, Mrs. Poppy's parlor looked out on the river. Betsy had never realized before how near the river was. From here she could see it clearly, and the bridge that spanned it, and the high bank rising on the other side covered with its fresh cloak of snow.

"Is the river frozen yet?" asked Betsy.

"It's mushy," Mrs. Poppy answered. "It thaws out in the middle of the day, but soon it will freeze for the winter. I hate to have it do that."

"Why?" Betsy asked.

"I like to look out and see it moving." After a moment Mrs. Poppy explained. "You see, I know that it's moving toward St. Paul, and that it joins the Mississippi there and keeps on going down to St. Louis and Memphis and New Orleans."

Betsy was surprised to hear that. Their own river! In which, beyond the town, they fished and bathed in summer and on which they skated in the winter. She had never thought of it going traveling. She told Mrs. Poppy so.

"It travels!" said Mrs. Poppy. "Like I used to do."

"You used to be an actress, didn't you?" asked Betsy.

"Yes. I sang in musical comedy."

"Why did you stop?"

"I stopped to marry Melborn Poppy and I've never regretted it."

"Do you like living in Deep Valley?"

"Yes," said Mrs. Poppy, but she said it slowly and without conviction. "I'm not acquainted here yet, of course. Living in a hotel you don't get acquainted easily. You don't have neighbors." She added the explanation quickly as though she had made it often to herself.

Betsy looked down at the melting mountain of whipped cream on her chocolate. She had a sudden sure knowledge of an amazing fact. Mrs. Poppy was lonesome. Lonesome in Deep Valley!

"Won't you have another cake?" Mrs. Poppy asked abruptly, gaily. "There are two frosted in chocolate, and two in pink, and two in vanilla. That means, we must have three apiece."

"I ate eighteen pancakes once," said Betsy, taking another cake. She looked out at the river and thought of Mrs. Poppy, an actress, traveling.

"I have an uncle who's an actor," she said.

Mrs. Poppy was much interested.

"Really? What's his name?"

"Keith Warrington. He's my mother's brother. He ran away from home because he didn't like his stepfather and he never came back."

She told Mrs. Poppy all she knew of Uncle Keith's story. Mrs. Poppy listened attentively.

"Keith Warrington!" she said. "I've never heard of him, although I have many friends in the profession. But do you know, Betsy, that if he's still an actor he's very likely to come to Deep Valley some day? Almost all the companies get here one time or another."

"That would be wonderful!" cried Betsy. "But I don't believe," she added thoughtfully, "that he would come to see us. You see, he doesn't know that grandpa and grandma have gone to California."

"We'll have to watch the programs. Keith Warrington," Mrs. Poppy said.

When they had finished their chocolate, Betsy and Mrs. Poppy looked over the magazines on Mrs. Poppy's table. They were all about the theatre with pictures in them of actors and actresses, and scenes from plays. Maude Adams in *The Little Minister*. E. H. Sothern in *An Enemy to the King*. James K. Hackett and Charlotte Walker in *The Crisis*, the Anna Held who took milk baths, and the matchless Lillian Russell.

Betsy and Mrs. Poppy were having such a good time that they were indignant when the cuckoo clock struck five.

"Oh dear me!" cried Mrs. Poppy. "I must take you to your father's. And I was going to show you my album, and play the graphophone. You'll have to come again.

"I know what we'll do," she said rapidly. "We'll have a party, a Christmas party here. You bring your friends Tacy and Tib and Winona. Do you think you could?"

"Of course!" cried Betsy. Her face shone.

"I'll write a note to your mother," Mrs. Poppy said. "For one day in Christmas vacation."

They planned about the party while Betsy took off the

fur-lined white slippers and put on her dry stockings and shoes. Mrs. Poppy put on her coat and cap and the two of them hurried out of the apartment and down the hall to the elevator.

Betsy liked going down in the elevator, although when it sank downward she seemed to be turned into liquid and flowing upward. She laughed out loud, and Mrs. Poppy said:

"If it weren't so late, we'd ride up and down two or three times."

But it was late. Lights had been lighted in the lobby. Outdoors the new snow gleamed in the radiance of Front Street.

Mrs. Poppy sniffed the cold fresh-smelling air.

"Feels like sleighs and sleighbells."

"Will you put sleighbells on the horseless carriage?"

"I'm afraid not," Mrs. Poppy laughed.

"We'll be coasting down the Big Hill soon," Betsy said. "I'm big enough to coast at night, on bobsleds now."

They talked busily all the way to the shoe store.

At home the story of Betsy's afternoon created much excitement.

"It was very kind of Mrs. Poppy," Mrs. Ray said. But there was something doubtful in her voice.

"Think of getting acquainted with a real live actress! Is she nice?" Julia asked.

"Yes," answered Betsy. "Very nice."

After a pause she addressed her mother.

"Mamma," she said. "Why don't you go down and call on Mrs. Poppy? Take your card case and drive down in the carriage and call, like you do on other ladies."

"She wouldn't care to have me, Betsy," Mrs. Ray said.

"Why not?" asked Betsy.

"Oh, she's different from us. It's sweet of her to take such an interest in you children, but she's different from us really. She's rich. And she lives in a hotel. And she's an actress," Mrs. Ray said.

Betsy remembered the feeling she had had that Mrs. Poppy was lonesome. She wished she could put that feeling into words, but any words, she feared, would sound absurd. She might have mentioned the doll in the rocking chair and Mrs. Poppy's little girl. But Mrs. Ray jumped up from the supper table and everyone got up. Julia went to the piano and Betsy helped Rena with the dishes. It was her turn.

IX

THE PINK STATIONERY

THE first snow melted. But the next one stayed on the ground. Another snow came, and another, and another, until everyone lost count. Snow loaded the bare arms of the maples; it lodged in the green crevices of firs; it threw sparkling shawls over the bare brown bushes shivering on Hill Street lawns.

The lawns themselves were billowing drifts, and so were the terraces, and so were the sidewalks. Men and boys came out with shovels to make Indian trails that children might follow to school. Along with the scraping of shovels came the frosty tinkle of sleighbells, as runners replaced wheels on the baker's wagon, cutters replaced carriages and buggies, and farm wagons creaked into town on runners. To steal a ride on those broad runners, or to hitch a sled thereto, was a delightful practice, shocking to parents.

Skates were sharpened; and down on the river, snow was swept from the ice. Up on Hill Street, in the Kelly front lawn, Paul was busy with a giant snowman. Freddie and Hobbie were building an Ice Palace in which they proposed to spend the winter . . . eat, sleep and everything, they said. Margaret and the Rivers children got out their small sleds, painted brightly with pictures of flowers, dogs, and

102

horses, and adventured harmlessly down the friendly slope of Hill Street.

Betsy, Tacy, and Tib got out their sleds, too. But with less enthusiasm than in previous years. It was fun to slide on the little sleds, yes; but what about bobsleds? Long, low, reckless, the bobsleds flew from the top of the Big Hill along a hard-packed frozen track in a thrilling sweep, almost to the slough. What about going out on bobsleds after supper, as Julia and Katie and their friends did?

"Please! You said last year we could."

"Please! We're old enough now."

"Please! All the kids our age stay up and go bobsled riding."

The same entreaties fell in the yellow Ray cottage and the rambling white Kelly house and the chocolate-colored house where Tib lived. It was a joint attack of exceptional vigor.

Jerry, home for Thanksgiving, helped them. Strange to say, he liked Betsy, Tacy, and Tib in spite of the nickels and dimes they had cost him. He had a fine big bob, and he and his friend Pin were taking Julia and Katie out coasting the night after Thanksgiving night.

"Let the kids come too," he urged Mrs. Ray. "Gosh, I'll be careful! There's a moon and the road is perfect."

"All right," said Mrs. Ray. "If you'll come in early."

When the other mothers heard that Mrs. Ray had given in, they gave in too.

Margaret watched, big-eyed, as Julia and Betsy put on their multitude of wraps. Mrs. Ray had two fur pieces that

she let them wear over their coats. As a finishing touch, over Betsy's hood and Julia's Tam o' Shanter, they wound bright knitted scarves called fascinators. These were stretched over their foreheads, crossed in back and tied around their necks.

Katie and Tacy and Tib arrived, as stiff with clothing as Julia and Betsy were.

"Gosh! Are you girls or mummies?" asked Jerry when he came in with Pin. Pin was called Pin because he was tall and thin. He was an expert on bobsleds.

Mr. and Mrs. Ray and Margaret went to the door to see them off.

"Come in early, so there'll be time to pop corn," Mrs. Ray said. If she mentioned popping corn, they always came in early. So she usually mentioned it.

They went out into the icy night.

The wastes of snow on the hill were ghostly in the moonlight. The stars were piercingly bright. They all helped pull the bobsled. It was a long way to the top of the Big Hill.

At the very top, near the Ekstroms' house, they stood looking out over the snowy roofs, the silent, snow-embedded town.

"It looks like something out of Whittier's 'Snowbound,'" Julia said.

Julia could always think of things like that to say.

They took their places on the bob. Jerry at the front with his feet on the steering bar, his knees hunched high and his firm hands grasping the rope that was first wound around his arms and wrists. The rest sat one behind the other, with arms around the waist of the one in front. Pin waited at the end.

"Feet up?"

"Hold tight, everybody."

"Ready?"

"Ready, go!"

Pin pushed off and leaped to his place.

Down, down, down, they sped. The bob was like an arrow flying an icy path. The stars sang overhead. The cold air slashed their faces. Down, down, down.

Past Betsy's house. The yellow windows blurred. Past Tacy's. But now the wind was so cold that their eyes were shut fast. Down, down, down. Block after block. Almost to the slough.

Like slow chords ending a piece of music the bob slackened speed, dragged to a stop.

The run down was worth the climb up, although that was long and cold. As they climbed they made jokes and called out to other coasting parties. The hill was well populated now. Julia and Katie waved to their friend Dorothy. Betsy, Tacy, and Tib saw Tom Slade and Herbert Humphreys. They were pleased to have Tom and Herbert see them out coasting after supper. Passing Tacy's house, and Betsy's, they waved to Paul and Margaret in the windows. At last for the second time they topped the Big Hill.

They went down twice, a third time . . .

On the third trip the bob tipped over. It wasn't a real accident, just a spill into snow. But when Betsy tried to stand up afterward, her ankle hurt. It was twisted, Jerry decided.

"Sit on the bobsled, Betsy," he said. "We'll haul you home."

Her ankle didn't hurt much, and Betsy felt important, especially when Jerry began to worry about facing her mother.

"Gosh!" he said. "The next time I ask you to go coasting she'll tell me to go way back and sit down."

"No, she won't," Julia answered. "She'll know it wasn't your fault."

Julia was right. Mrs. Ray was reassuring when Jerry burst in with his explanations and apologies and Betsy followed, limping, on Pin's arm.

"Don't worry," she said. "It isn't a bobsled party without a spill or two."

Her tone was cheerful. But her eyes were a little anxious. The truth was, Mrs. Ray didn't like bobsled parties. None of the mothers did.

After Mr. Ray had bandaged Betsy's ankle and pronounced it a trifling sprain, Mrs. Ray was as gay as a bird. She was so thankful that nothing worse had happened.

"Come on! Pop your corn," she said. "There are apples to roast, too."

Julia and Katie, Jerry and Pin repaired to the kitchen. Laughter rose above the sound of popcorn bouncing in a shaker. Tacy and Tib put apples to roast on the back of the hard-coal heater that sat like a rosy smiling god in a corner of the back parlor.

Betsy sat on the back-parlor sofa with her foot on a pillow. Jerry came in often to see how she felt.

"Gosh, she was a good soldier, Mrs. Ray!" he kept saying.

Betsy felt heroic.

The big pan of fluffy buttered popcorn was brought in and passed. Julia went to the piano, and everybody sang. They sang *Navajo* and *Hiawatha* and *Bedelia*, and Jerry and Julia sang a duet called, "Tell me, pretty maiden."

Mr. Ray smoked his pipe and looked pleased. He liked people to have a good time at his house.

At last Mrs. Ray played the piano, and Julia and Jerry, Katie and Pin danced a waltz. They pushed back the dining-room table and had a Virginia Reel. Mr. Ray joined in, and so did Tacy, and Tib, and Rena who came in smiling from the kitchen. The blue plates on the plate rail danced, too. Only Betsy could not dance because of her foot. But she had a good time anyway, feeling heroic.

"As soon as I get back to Cox," Jerry told her when he said good-by, "I'm going to send you a present. What would you like? A postcard album?"

A postcard album! It was just what she had been wanting.

Betsy was out of school for a week, but she didn't mind very much. It was pleasant to snuggle down in bed when she heard the hard-coal heater being shaken down in the morning. Julia and Margaret had to get up; they hurried into their clothes over the open register that brought heat into their bedroom. Betsy didn't need to hurry.

She hobbled downstairs late and spent most of the day on the back-parlor sofa. She liked to watch the red flames flickering behind the isinglass windows of the stove. After the postcard album came . . . for Jerry sent it! It had leather covers and the seal of Cox School on it . . . she enjoyed putting in her collection of postcards. Postcards from her grandmother in California and from various uncles and aunts, from her father that time he went to St. Paul and from Tib when she went to visit in Milwaukee.

She had two new books to read for she had been to the library just the Saturday before the bobsled party. Miss Sparrow had picked them out for her. *The Water Babies* by Charles Kingsley and *Pickwick Papers* by Charles Dickens.

When she grew tired of reading she played paper dolls.

Betsy hardly ever played with her paper dolls any more. Yet she loved them; she didn't want to throw them away. And when she was sick, or kept indoors for any reason, she got them out and played with them.

At last, however, she grew sick of paper dolls, too.

Her mother was going out that day. She and Margaret were going to the high school to hear Julia sing at the Literary Society program. It was Rena's afternoon off.

"I'm glad Tacy and Tib always come in after school," Mrs. Ray said. "You won't be alone very long."

She put out a plate of cookies to be ready for Tacy and Tib, and she and Margaret kissed Betsy and went out. Old Mag, hitched to the cutter, was waiting in front of the house. Mr. Ray had left her there at noon.

Betsy waved from the back parlor window, and when the cutter had vanished down Hill Street and the sound of the sleighbells had died, she kept on staring out of doors. The

street was empty. There was nothing to see but snow glistening in the sunshine.

Betsy stared a long time. Then she hobbled upstairs to her desk and brought down one of those tablets marked "Ray's Shoe Store. Wear Queen Quality Shoes."

When Tacy and Tib came in after school, they found her on the sofa, scribbling furiously. Her braids had come loose, her cheeks were red, and there was a smudge on her nose.

"I'm just finishing a story," she said. "Would you like to hear it?"

"You bet. Swell," said Tacy and Tib.

"It'll be done in a jiff."

Tacy and Tib took off their wraps and stowed them away in the closet. They helped themselves to cookies and sat down in comfortable chairs.

By that time Betsy was ready. She sat up and cleared her throat.

"It's a very good story," she said.

She announced the title sonorously.

"Flossie's Accident."

Betsy liked to read her stories aloud and she read them like an actress. She made her voice low and thrillingly deep. She made it shake with emotion. She laughed mockingly and sobbed wildly when the occasion required.

And she was right about this story. It was a good one. Tacy soon stopped munching cookies and leaned forward in excitement. Tib cried real tears. She always cried real tears in the most flattering manner when Betsy's stories were sad.

Flossie's Accident was very, very sad.

It was about a girl named Flossie who was hurt in a bobsled accident. The accident was something like Betsy's, but Flossie didn't look like Betsy. She had long black ringlets, and big black eyes, and a dead white skin with lips as red as blood. She was dressed all in fluffy white fur, white coat and cap, mittens, boots and everything. She was white as a snowdrift and very beautiful.

When the bobsled turned over, her head was broken off. She was still alive and beautiful, but she didn't have a head.

Her father and mother didn't like the way she looked.

"You are no child of ours," they said, and cruelly shut the door in her face.

Bad boys and girls threw snowballs at her. They laughed at her and chased her.

Holding her head by its long black ringlets, she ran along the frozen river.

"Could she see with it?" Tib interrupted.

"Oh, yes. She could see. She held it up like a lantern."

"Could she hear?"

"Yes. She could hear too. She couldn't eat though. It wouldn't have been practical for her to eat."

"I should think she'd have starved to death," said Tib.

Betsy did not answer.

Flossie followed the river as far as St. Paul. It met the Mississippi there. She followed it to St. Louis, to Memphis, to New Orleans. Forlorn and outcast she wandered everywhere.

She shunned towns and cities, for the people in them laughed at her; or worse still, they ran from her in terror.

But after dark she liked to look in at the windows of houses where happy families lived.

Sometimes she saw good things to eat on the tables. Baked beans and brown bread. Or stewed chicken with dumplings. Or pancakes with maple syrup. She looked at them longingly, for she was very hungry.

She saw children romping beside the hard-coal heaters and husbands kissing their wives.

Flossie's heart almost broke when she saw scenes like that. She couldn't ever get married without a head. She couldn't have children. In fact, there was nothing Flossie could do. She couldn't teach school. She couldn't clerk in a store. She couldn't do anything but wander.

So she kept on wandering.

"Did she wear her fur coat all the time?" Tib wanted to know.

"Yes," answered Betsy. "She wore it year in and year out."

"It must have been pretty hot in the summer time."

"Sweltering. There was one good thing about that coat though. It never got dirty. Wherever she went or whatever she did, it stayed as white as snow."

Flossie wandered and wandered, as the story ran on and on. Her adventures were many and excruciatingly sad. At last she hid in a ship and crossed the ocean. When she got off, she was in Greece.

She was walking along a road there (carrying her head, of course), when she met a handsome youth. He had blond hair and blue eyes and tanned rosy cheeks.

"He reminds me of Herbert Humphreys," said Tib.

"His name," said Betsy, "was Chauncey."

Chauncey did not laugh and jeer at Flossie as other people did. He stopped and asked her kindly what her trouble was.

"You look like the *Winged Victory*," he said.

She did, too, although she did not have wings.

Flossie told him her story.

"Come with me," said Chauncey.

Taking her by the hand, he led her to the top of a mountain. They looked down on olive groves and the blue Mediterranean Sea.

He built a fire of cedar boughs and when smoke began to rise he said a prayer to the gods and goddesses. He was sort of a god himself. He took Flossie's head by its ringlets and swung it back and forth in the smoke from his fire. Then he clapped it on her swanlike neck, and it fastened there at once. She was just as beautiful as she had been before the bobsled accident. They got married and went to live on the Island of Delos, and they had ten children, five boys and five girls.

"That's the end of the story," said Betsy, closing the tablet.

"Betsy! It's wonderful!" cried Tacy.

"It's the best story you ever wrote," said Tib.

"It's the best story I ever heard in my life."

"That poor Flossie!"

Tacy jumped to her feet.

"Betsy," she said, excitedly, yet earnestly, "your stories ought to be published. I've been thinking that for a long time although I never mentioned it before."

Betsy looked at Tacy deeply. It was strange, she thought, that Tacy should say that for she had been thinking the very thing herself.

"They're just as good as the stories in the *Ladies' Home Journal,*" said Tacy. "Don't you think so, Tib?"

"Better," Tib said.

"How do people get stories published, do you suppose?"

"I think," said Betsy, "they just send them to the magazines."

"Why don't you send this one then?"

"Maybe I will," said Betsy. Her heart leaped up like a little fish in a bowl. "I haven't any good paper though."

"My sister Mary has some," said Tacy. "A box of lovely pink stationery. Got it for her birthday. She'd give me some, I think. And since she isn't at home, I'll just take it."

"You mean . . . right now?"

"Right now. We'll copy that story and get it off."

"I'll print it for you," cried Tib. Tib was famous for her printing.

Tacy seized her coat and overshoes and ran out of the house. Tib opened the bookcase desk and spread Betsy's tablet on it. She took Betsy's pencil out to the kitchen and sharpened it to an exquisite point. Betsy waited, feeling queer inside.

Tacy came back breathless with the pink stationery.

"I didn't dare take more than one sheet. Do you think you can get the story on, Tib?"

"I think so," said Tib. "I'll print small."

She set to work with painstaking care. While she labored, Betsy and Tacy made plans.

"Betsy," said Tacy solemnly, "you're going to be famous after that story is published."

"How much do you suppose I'll be paid for it?" Betsy asked.

"Oh, probably a hundred dollars."

"What shall we spend it for?"

"Let's see! What!"

They decided to buy silk dresses with hats to match. A blue one for Tacy (because she had red hair). A pink one for Betsy and a yellow one for Tib.

"We'll wear them to Mrs. Poppy's party," said Betsy.

"We'll wear them to the next matinee Winona takes us to. They'll look fine in a box," Tacy said.

"See here," said Tib, sounding worried. "It's going to be hard to squeeze this story on."

"Oh, you can squeeze it on," said Betsy.

"I'll have to print awfully small."

"It doesn't matter," said Tacy. "They'll be so anxious to know how that story's coming out that they'll use a microscope on it, if they have to."

So Tib persisted, and by printing very, very, very small she got all the story on the sheet of pink stationery, down to the last word.

"I saw the Lord's Prayer printed on a dime one time," said Betsy. "It looked a good deal like that."

They put the pink stationery into an envelope and addressed it to the *Ladies' Home Journal*, Independence Square, Philadelphia, Pa. Betsy found a stamp and stuck it on.

"I'll put it in the mailbox on my way home," said Tib, sighing with content.

They all sat on the sofa then, while the sky, behind brown tree trunks, took on the tint of mother-of-pearl, matching the tint of the snow. They planned about the silk dresses and hats.

Betsy and Tacy and Tib were twelve years old now, and when they made plans like that they didn't quite believe them. But they liked to make them anyhow.

X

CHRISTMAS SHOPPING

OW long does it take a letter to go to Philadelphia?" Betsy asked her father that night at supper.

"Two or three days," he replied.

"Whom do you know in Philadelphia?" asked Julia, stressing the "whom."

"Never mind," said Betsy. "Someone important."

"The King of Spain maybe," said her father. He was teasing. For when Betsy and Tacy and Tib were only ten years old and didn't know any better, they had written a letter to the King of Spain. They had received an answer, too.

Betsy laughed at her father's joke, but underneath the table she was counting on her fingers.

Three days for the story to go, a day for the editor to read it, three days for his letter and the hundred dollar bill to return.

The transaction could be completed in a week, she told Tacy and Tib next day. But a week passed, and another, without any word about Flossie.

Betsy was back in school, of course. At the end of the second week, school closed for the Christmas vacation. That meant that Betsy, Tacy, and Tib had an important engagement. For years on the first day of Christmas vacation they had gone shopping together.

"Let's take Winona this year," Tib suggested.

Winona had come to be quite a friend of theirs. They often stopped after school to slide down her terrace, a particularly steep and hazardous one, or to play show in her dining room. Winona loved to play show; she was always the villainess.

"I'd like to take her," said Tacy. "She'd be pretty surprised, I guess, at the way we shop."

"She certainly would be," said Betsy, and all of them laughed.

"You see," Betsy explained to Winona when they invited her, "we usually make our Christmas presents, or else our mothers buy them for us . . . the ones we give away, I mean."

"Then why do you go shopping?" Winona asked.

"We go shopping to shop," said Tacy.

The three of them smiled. Winona looked mystified.

"We've done it the same way ever since we were children," said Betsy. "We always take ten cents apiece, and we always buy just the same things."

"What do you buy?"

"You'll see," said Betsy, "if you want to come along."

They liked to tease Winona because she was such a tease herself.

Winona's black eyes snapped.

"I'll come," she said.

They made plans to meet the next day at a quarter after two. Betsy didn't want to leave home until the mail came.

(She and Tacy and Tib were watching every mail for her hundred dollars.)

Every day they changed their minds about how they would spend it. First they had decided on the silk dresses and hats. Then they changed to a Shetland pony, and now it was a trip to Niagara Falls.

They were planning the trip to the Falls with great enthusiasm when Mr. Goode, the postman, came into sight.

They swooped down upon him, three abreast. (They had been waiting on Betsy's hitching block.)

"I haven't a blessed thing for any of you," he said. "What are you looking for, anyway? Another letter from a king?"

He was like Betsy's father; he couldn't forget that letter from the King of Spain.

"This is a business letter, Mr. Goode," Betsy said.

"Money in it, too," said Tib. "A hundred dollars, we expect."

"I'll be careful with it when it comes," said Mr. Goode.

They hurried down to call for Winona, running and sliding in the icy street.

Winona was waiting in front of her house wearing a crimson coat and hat. She looked like a rakish cardinal against the snow.

"Does it matter," she asked, swinging her pocket book, "if I take more than ten cents?"

"Of course it matters. It isn't allowed." Betsy, Tacy, and Tib were noisily indignant.

"That's all I've got anyway," Winona grinned. "Just asked for fun."

"You go way back and sit down," Tacy said.

They started off down town.

The fluffy white drifts had packed into hard ramparts guarding the sidewalks. The four had to keep to the sidewalks after they passed Lincoln Park. The streets were crowded with sleighs and cutters. Chiming bells added to the Christmassy feeling in the air.

Front Street was very Christmassy. Evergreen boughs and holly wreaths, red bells and mistletoe sprays surrounded displays of tempting merchandise in all the store windows. In one window a life-sized Santa Claus with a brimming pack on his back was halfway into a papier-mâché chimney.

"Look here!" said Winona, stopping to admire. "This will tickle the little kids."

"The *little* kids?"

"The ones that believe in Santa Claus."

"Gee whiz!" said Betsy. "I didn't think we were *little* kids any more. I thought we were twelve years old; didn't you, Tacy?"

"I was under that impression," said Tacy.

"Why, we are! What do you mean?" asked Tib.

Winona knew what they meant.

"Are you trying to tell me," she asked, "that you believe in Santa Claus?"

"Certainly, we do!"

"Well, of all . . ." began Winona. She stopped, words failing her, and looked at them with a scorn which changed to suspicion as she viewed their broadly smiling faces.

"I expect to believe in Santa Claus when I'm in high school," said Tacy.

"I expect to believe in him when I'm grown up and married," said Betsy. "I hear him on the roof every year; don't you, Tacy?"

"Sure I do. And I've seen the reindeer go past the bedroom window, lots of times."

"You see," explained Tib. "We've made an agreement about him. We've crossed our hearts and even signed a paper."

"You three take the cake!" said Winona. "All right. I believe in him too."

They came to Cook's Book Store.

"We start here," said Betsy.

"Is that where we spend our dimes?" asked Winona.

"Mercy, no! We don't spend them for hours yet. We just shop. Choose a present."

"I know what I'm going to choose," said Betsy. "*Little Men*. I got *Little Women* last year."

They went in and said hello to Mr. Cook. His bright eyes looked out sharply under his silky toupee.

"You never pass me up, do you?" he said. He said it good naturedly though.

"This year we brought Winona Root. She's another customer for you, Mr. Cook," said Tib.

"Customer!" said Mr. Cook. "Customer! Oh well, look around."

They looked around. They looked around thoroughly. They read snatches in the Christmas books. They studied the directions on all the games. Tacy chose a pencil set, and Tib chose colored crayons.

"Choose! Go ahead and choose! Choose whatever you

like," they urged Winona hospitably.

Winona chose a book about Indians.

They went next door to the harness and saddle maker's shop. There wasn't much to choose here, just whips and buggy robes. Getting into the spirit of the game, Winona cracked a dozen whips before she chose one. Betsy and Tacy chose robes, with landscapes printed on them.

There was a tall wooden horse standing in the window. It was almost seven feet tall, dapple gray, with flashing glass eyes and springy mane and tail. Every year the harness and saddle maker let Tib sit on the horse.

He looked at her sadly now as she put her foot in a stirrup and swung nimbly upward.

"If the horseless carriages keep coming to town, I'll have to take that fellow down," he said.

That gave Tib an idea.

"I know what I'll choose then," she cried. "I'll choose this horse. I'll put him up in our back yard and all of us can ride him."

"Tib! What fun!"

"I wish I'd thought to choose him."

"It's a spiffy idea, Tib!" Betsy cried.

Winona had an idea even spiffier.

"Let's go choose horseless carriages," she suggested nonchalantly. "The hardware-store man sells them."

For a moment Betsy, Tacy, and Tib were dazzled by this brilliant plan. Then Tib scrambled down from the horse. Saying good-by to the melancholy harness and saddle maker, they raced to the hardware store.

Sure enough, there was a horseless carriage on display there. They inspected it from every angle, and the curly-haired hardware-store man let them sit in it for awhile. He was very obliging. All four of them chose it, and while they were in the store they looked at skates and bicycles.

"I could use a new sled," said Winona.

So they looked at sleds too.

At the Lion Department store they shopped even more extensively. There were many departments, and they visited them all. The busy clerks paid little attention to them. They wandered happily about.

They chose rhinestone side combs, jeweled hat pins, gay pompadour pouffs. They chose fluffy collars and belts and pocket books. They chose black lace stockings and taffeta petticoats and embroidered corset covers.

It was hard to tear themselves away but they did so at last. They went to the drug store where they sniffed assiduously. They sniffed every kind of perfume in the store before they chose, finally, rose and lilac and violet, and new-mown hay.

"I want new-mown hay because it's the kind Mrs. Poppy uses," Betsy said.

"Mrs. Poppy!" exclaimed Tacy. "That reminds me of her party. We'd better go to the jewelry store and choose some jewels."

"Goodness, yes!" said Betsy. "I need a diamond ring to wear to that party."

They hurried to the jewelry store. The clerks there weren't very helpful, however. They wouldn't let them try on diamond rings, or necklaces, or bracelets. They wouldn't even let them handle the fat gold watches, with doves engraved on the sides, which looked so fashionable pinned to a shirtwaist.

"They act this way every year," said Betsy to Winona. "Let's go to the toy shop. That's the nicest, anyhow."

The toy shop was what they had all been waiting for. They had been holding it off in order to have it still ahead of them. But the time for it had come at last.

At the toy shop it was difficult to choose. In blissful indecision they circled the table of dolls. Yellow-haired dolls with blue dresses, black-haired dolls with pink dresses, baby dolls, boy dolls, picaninny dolls.

Betsy, Tacy, Tib, and Winona had stopped playing with dolls, except on days when they were sick, perhaps, or when stormy weather kept them indoors. Yet choosing dolls was the most fun of all. They liked the dolls' appurtenances too.

They inspected doll dishes, doll stoves, sets of shiny doll tinware, doll parlor sets.

There was one magnificent doll house, complete even to the kitchen. Winona asked the price of it.

"Twenty-five dollars? Hmm! Well, it's worth it," said Winona thoughtfully, swinging her pocket book.

When they were through with the dolls they began on

the other toys. Trains of cars, jumping jacks, woolly animals on wheels.

"Gee!" said Winona at last. "I'm getting tired. When do we spend our dimes?"

"Dimes!" said the clerk who had told her the price of the doll's house. "Dimes!" She settled her eye glasses on the thin ridge of her nose and looked at the four severely.

When she had turned away, Betsy whispered, "Right now!"

"I hope," said Winona, "we spend them for something to eat."

"We don't. But after we've spent them, we go to call on our fathers. And you can't call on four fathers, without being invited out to Heinz's restaurant for ice cream."

"I suppose not," Winona agreed. "Well, what do we buy then?"

Betsy turned and led the way to the far end of the store.

There on a long table Christmas tree ornaments were set out for sale. There were boxes and boxes full of them, their colors mingling in bewildering iridescence. There were large fragile balls of vivid hues, there were gold and silver balls; there were tinsel angels, shining harps and trumpets, gleaming stars.

"Here," said Betsy, "here we buy."

She looked at Winona, bright-eyed, and Winona looked from her to the resplendent table.

"Nothing," Tacy tried to explain, "is so much like Christmas as a Christmas-tree ornament."

"You get a lot for ten cents," said Tib.

They gave themselves then with abandon to the sweet delight of choosing. It was almost pain to choose. Each fragile bauble was gayer, more enchanting than the last. And now they were not only choosing, they were buying. What each one chose she would take home; she would see it on the Christmas tree; she would see it year after year, if she were lucky and it did not break.

They walked around and around the table, touching softly with mittened hands.

Betsy at last chose a large red ball. Tacy chose an angel. Tib chose a rosy Santa Claus. Winona chose a silver trumpet.

They yielded their dimes and the lady with the eye glasses wrapped up four packages. Betsy, Tacy, Tib, and Winona went out into the street. The afternoon was drawing to a pallid close. Soon the street lamps would be lighted.

"Which father shall we call on first?" Winona asked.

"Mine is nearest Heinz's Restaurant," said Betsy.

They walked to Ray's Shoe Store, smiling, holding Christmas in their hands.

XI

MRS. POPPY'S PARTY

TO GO from Before Christmas to After Christmas was like climbing and descending a high glittering peak. Christmas, of course, sat at the top. The trip down was usually more abrupt and far less pleasurable than the long climb up, but not this year. For this year, the After Christmas held Mrs. Poppy's party.

Before Christmas started with the shopping expedition. Or even earlier, with the school Christmas Entertainment. The carols, the pungent evergreens, made their first appearance there. The Sunday School Christmas Entertainment followed, with speaking pieces and presents.

After the shopping trip one climbed through mists of secrecy . . . at the Ray house, one did. There was whispering and giggling. Doors were slammed when one approached. Rena was working with crepe paper in her bedroom; Julia kept whisking her sewing bag out of sight. Everyone cautioned everyone else not to look here or look there.

"Betsy, don't open the lowest sideboard drawer."

"Don't look in the right-hand upper drawer of my bureau."

"Keep out of the downstairs closet!"

Betsy knew so many secrets that she was afraid to speak

for fear one would pop out like the jack-in-the-box she had seen in the toy shop.

What if she should accidentally mention the silver cake basket her father was giving to her mother? Or the burned wood handkerchief box Julia was making for her father? Or, above all, Margaret's talking doll? Everyone was waiting to see Margaret's eyes when the doll said "mamma" on Christmas morning.

Margaret's eyes were big in her little serious face. The long black lashes seemed not so much to shade them as to make them bigger and brighter. They were big and bright enough the night her father brought the tree home. It was a feathery hemlock and smelled deliciously when Betsy and Margaret visited it in the woodshed.

On Christmas Eve it was brought indoors. It was set up in a corner of the dining room and a star was fixed on its crest. Strings of popcorn and cranberries were woven through its branches that were hung with colored balls.

Betsy put on the red ball she had bought on this year's Christmas shopping trip. She looked for the harp she had bought last year, and the angel from the year before. When all was ready, the candles were lighted. Bits of live flame danced all over the tree.

Betsy's mother went to the piano then. They all sang together. *Oh, Little Town of Bethlehem. It Came Upon the Midnight Clear.* And *Silent Night*, most beloved of all.

"Let's read about the Cratchits' Christmas dinner," Mr. Ray said. He always said it.

He crossed his legs and got out his pipe and Betsy went

to the bookcase for Dickens' *Christmas Carol*. Betsy read aloud about the Cratchits' goose, and Tiny Tim. Margaret pretended to read . . . (she knew it by heart) . . . *'Twas the Night Before Christmas*. Julia read the story of Jesus' birth out of the *Book of Luke*.

The stockings were hung around the hard-coal heater. Mr. and Mrs. Ray and Rena all hung stockings too. In some families, Betsy had heard, only children hung stockings. But it was not so in the Ray house. Mr. Ray complained loudly of the smallness of his sock.

The lamps were turned low and they scurried around in the dimness putting presents into one another's stockings. One could not avoid seeing knobby bundles being stuffed into one's own stocking.

"I don't peek; do I?" asked Margaret, trotting about.

"I should say you don't," Mrs. Ray replied.

"I'd be ashamed to, wouldn't I?" Margaret continued.

"You certainly would."

"I wouldn't," said Mr. Ray and pretended to make a dash for his sock. Margaret caught him around the knees. Julia and Betsy pinioned his arms, while Rena screamed and laughed at once.

"Lord-a-mercy! Lord-a-mercy!"

"Stop it! Stop it!" cried Mrs. Ray, pulling them apart. "Bob, you behave and go down cellar and get us some cider. These children must get to bed sometime tonight. We have to give Santa Claus a chance."

Santa Claus, of course!

After Julia and Betsy and Margaret went upstairs, when

the lamp had been blown out, they looked out the window. They saw the snowy roof of Tacy's house, the snowy silent hill, the waiting stars.

"No Santa Claus yet," they said.

But after they got into bed they began to hear him.

"Margaret! Don't you hear something on the roof?"

"I think it's reindeer. Don't you, Betsy?"

"It can't be yet. Papa and mamma haven't gone to bed."

"Julia, he's so fat and our chimney's so small, how can he get down?"

"He gets down. It's magic."

"What would he do . . ." Margaret breathed hard with daring, "if we ran downstairs and caught him?"

"Better not do that. He'd never come again."

"I won't." Margaret shivered in delighted apprehension. For the dozenth time she snuggled down in bed.

Mrs. Ray called upstairs.

"Children! Stop talking!"

"Children! Get some sleep! Remember tomorrow's Christmas."

Remember tomorrow's Christmas! As though they could forget it!

Margaret waked up first. It was the first year she had waked ahead of Betsy. In her little high-necked, long-sleeved flannel night gown, she pattered through Rena's bedroom, downstairs.

"Margaret! Go back to bed! It's only four."

On the second trip Betsy went with her. On the third trip Julia went too. It was still as black as night, but now the three of them jumped into the big bed with their mother.

They cuddled there, laughing and giggling, while their father in his dressing gown shook down and filled the hard-coal heater.

"My! My! You ought to see what I see!" he called out over the sound of rattling coal.

"Has Santa Claus come?" Margaret's fingers were clutching Betsy's arm.

"Sure, he's come."

"Can we get up? When can we get up?"

"Not until the room gets warm."

Betsy's mother got up though. Rena was up already. The smell of coffee and sausages was drifting through the house.

Julia got dressed. But Betsy and Margaret stayed in bed imagining things.

They did not imagine the glory of that moment when they opened the bedroom door and saw the stockings, around the glowing stove, swimming in Christmas-tree light!

Margaret stared at the yellow-haired doll peeping from her stocking. She walked toward it slowly.

"Take it out, Margaret," called her mother, while the others waited breathlessly.

She took it out.

"Squeeze it, Margaret."

She squeezed it, looking down with a grave face.

"Harder!"

She squeezed it harder, and the yellow-haired doll spoke. "Mamma! Mamma!" said the doll in a light quick voice.

"Mamma! Mamma!" cried Margaret, her eyes like Christmas stars.

That was the sparkling summit of Christmas at the Ray house.

The descent was gay. Stockings were unpacked down to the orange and the dollar from Grandpa Ray that were always found at the bottom. There were presents for everyone, beautiful presents, and joke presents too.

Julia got a postage stamp (for a letter to Jerry) tastefully wrapped in a hat box. Margaret got one butternut with a card signed "Squirrel, Esquire." Betsy got one of her own much-chewed pencils "With Sympathy from William Shakespeare." Mr. Ray got a pan of burned biscuits. Rena had been saving them ever since she burned them almost a week before.

Mr. Ray's antics with those biscuits made Rena laugh until she cried. He acted as though he did not know they were a joke; he acted as though he thought he was expected to eat them. He chewed and chewed, looking solemn and worried, while the others rocked with mirth.

"Lord-a-mercy, I've got to get that turkey on!" said Rena at last.

"And my pies!" cried Mrs. Ray jumping up lightly to kiss Mr. Ray for the silver cake basket.

Everyone kissed everyone else, saying "Thank You." And Betsy dressed and ran over to show Tacy *Little Men.* (Mr. Cook must have told her father she wanted it.)

The Kelly house was a happy bedlam. Betsy stayed there until the family went to church. Then she went on to Tib's to feast on Christmas cookies, cut in the shapes of stars and animals and frosted with colored sugar.

Dinner came at one o'clock sharp. Full of turkey and turkey dressing, gravy and cranberry sauce, mashed turnips, creamed onions, celery, rolls, and mince and pumpkin pie, people either took naps or went sliding. Betsy, Tacy, and Tib went sliding. So did Margaret and all the younger children.

Everyone out on the hill had something new. A new sled, or a new cap, or new red knitted mittens. They slid and slid until purple shadows fell across the snow. Betsy came in at last to read beside the fire. Turkey sandwiches, made by her father, ended the day.

Usually she went to bed on Christmas night feeling very much on the other side of the glorious holiday peak. But not this year. She was almost as excited as though it were Christmas Eve, for the next day came Mrs. Poppy's party.

The note of invitation had arrived several days before. It was written in a large childish handwriting on rich blue paper, heavily scented with new-mown hay perfume.

"Of course you may go. It's very nice of her." But Mrs. Ray's voice still held that note of reservation. Why was it? Betsy wondered. Mrs. Poppy wasn't any different from anybody else except that she was nicer than most.

"I wish," said Betsy slowly, "you were acquainted with Mrs. Poppy. I think she'd like to get acquainted with you."

"P'shaw!" said Mrs. Ray. "She isn't interested in anything here. She's in the Twin Cities, half the time. We haven't anything in common. If I thought she was lonesome, I'd go to see her, of course." Her tone added, "I'm sure she isn't though."

Julia broke into the conversation. She had just come in from skating with Jerry, at home for the Christmas vacation.

"I'm longing to meet her. Jerry says she was a very fine singer. She sang in *Erminie*. That lullaby you used to sing to us."

"Oh, really?" Mrs. Ray seemed interested in this. But when Betsy pressed her, asking, "*Will* you go to see her, mamma?" she answered, "Maybe. Sometime," in that tone which meant "Probably not."

Mrs. Kelly, Mrs. Muller, and Mrs. Root seemed to feel much as Mrs. Ray did. But fortunately Tacy and Tib and Winona were allowed to go to the party.

They were trig and trim down to their polished shoes when they pushed through the swinging door at the Melborn Hotel. They wore their best hats and big vivid hair ribbons; best dresses too, under their winter coats.

Betsy took the lead. It was hard to take the lead from Winona but she did it because she had visited Mrs. Poppy before.

"This is the *Winged Victory*," she said, pausing by the statue on the landing.

"The one Flossie looked like?" Tib asked, staring up.

"Yes. Only Flossie didn't have wings."

"Who was Flossie?"

"She's in a story I wrote," Betsy answered quickly. They hadn't told Winona about the pink stationery. They were afraid she would tease them if the hundred dollars didn't come. And it still hadn't come. They had stopped making plans about it.

Mrs. Poppy opened the door to them, smiling radiantly. She looked like a big peony in a peony-pink silk dress. She wore a sprig of holly pinned to her shoulder.

"Merry Christmas!" she cried.

"Merry Christmas!" cried Betsy, Tacy, Tib, and Winona. They surged into the hall.

They took off their wraps in the blue bedroom and Betsy shot a look at Minnie's doll. It looked faded and old in the little rocking chair beside Mrs. Poppy's bed. She wondered whether Minnie had been given that doll for a Christmas present and how long ago. She wondered whether Mr. and Mrs. Poppy had grown used to not having Minnie around on Christmas morning.

Suddenly she wished urgently that she had brought Mrs. Poppy a present. Why hadn't she thought of it? Why hadn't her mother, usually quick with such ideas, had this one? Or Mrs. Muller . . . she might have sent some Christmas cookies. She was always sending people boxes of her cookies. But no one had sent anything.

"We've got to do something about Mrs. Poppy," Betsy thought so vigorously that she found herself frowning into the mirror. She made herself smile, and presently she felt like smiling.

Mr. Poppy's den had a sprig of mistletoe over the door.

"I put it there," said Mrs. Poppy, looking roguish.

In the parlor there were wreaths at the windows. A fat

glittering tree stood on a table.

"There are packages for all of you. They have your names on," Mrs. Poppy said.

Her eyes brimmed with pleasure as they jostled one another, hunting for their gifts.

They all received perfume. Rose and lilac and violet and new-mown hay.

"You may exchange with one another," Mrs. Poppy said. "I knew you wanted those four scents, but I didn't know which wanted which."

"But how did you know we wanted perfume at all?" they cried, exchanging.

"The man at the drug store told me. I told him whom I was buying it for and he seemed to know all about you."

"He does! He does!" They went off into gales of laughter.

"It's the first perfume I ever had, Mrs. Poppy," Tacy said.

"Me too," said Tib, sniffing her beloved rose.

"I've had perfume, but never lilac," said Winona.

"Now I'll smell just like you," Betsy said.

Rapturously they doused themselves and each other.

They played the graphophone; and Mrs. Poppy played the piano for them to sing. The first thing they knew they were giving a sort of entertainment. Betsy and Tacy sang their Cat Duet; it was a duet they often sang at school. Winona sang a very sad song about *The Baggage Car Ahead*. And Tib danced her Baby Dance.

She had danced her Baby Dance many times since she danced it first at a school entertainment. Betsy and Tacy knew the music so well they could sing it. They sang it now, for Tib to dance by in Mrs. Poppy's parlor.

Tib loved to dance, and Tib was like Julia . . . she loved to perform. Smilingly, she lifted her skirts by the edges, ran and made her pirouette. There were five different steps in the Baby Dance, each one to be done thirty-two times. She did them all triumphantly, and when her audience applauded at the end, she ran back to the center of the room to curtsey and kiss her hands, as she had seen Little Eva do.

Mrs. Poppy was enchanted with the Baby Dance.

"Thank you so much for doing it," she said, ruffling Tib's yellow curls.

"I like to do it," said Tib. "I'm getting a little tired of it though. I wish I knew a new dance."

"Do you?" Mrs. Poppy cried. "I could easily teach you one, if your mother would like me to. I know quite a lot of steps."

Winona played a tune, and Mrs. Poppy lifted her peony-pink skirts. Her feet were small and dainty in slippers the color of her dress. In spite of her weight Mrs. Poppy danced lightly, with a skill which fascinated Tib.

When the maid knocked, Mrs. Poppy cried, "Mercy me! I haven't even set the table."

They all helped her spread the white embroidered cloth and put out the hand-painted cups and saucers and plates. The maid came in smiling, and there was ice cream today, in addition to the frosted cakes and the pot of hot chocolate and the bowl of whipped cream.

They had a gay time eating the refreshments.

Mrs. Poppy asked them how the man in the drug store had happened to know what kinds of perfume they wanted. They told her about their Christmas shopping, and she laughed and laughed, and so did they. They told her all about their Christmases, too.

Now and then Betsy looked out to the river, white and still in its blanket of snow. She wondered whether Mrs. Poppy missed its restless journeying down to St. Paul to meet the Mississippi. She thought about Mrs. Poppy's journeyings and her acting and her singing. She thought about Uncle Keith.

She was glad when Mrs. Poppy sent Tacy and Tib and Winona out to ride in the elevator, and said in a lowered voice:

"Betsy, I want to talk with you a minute. I want you to know that I'm trying to find your uncle. I'm making inquiries and looking for his name in the casts of all the plays Mr. Poppy books. Don't mention it to your mother yet. I don't want her to be disappointed if I haven't any luck."

"Mrs. Poppy!" cried Betsy. "How kind of you! Mamma would be so glad."

She wished she could say that her mother was coming soon to get acquainted but she knew she couldn't. She did repeat, though, what Julia had said about wanting to meet her.

"She's the one who sings?" asked Mrs. Poppy with vivid interest. "Why, I'd love to have her come! Maybe I could help her."

Her blue eyes suddenly misted over.

"Wouldn't it be wonderful, Betsy," she said, "if I could *help* here in Deep Valley? Help children like Tib and your sister with the things I know how to do? I've studied with good masters. I know how to dance, and something about music. It would make me feel I *belonged* if I could be of use here."

Betsy did not answer. She was a talker, her family always said, but sometimes when she most wanted to talk she couldn't say a word.

She looked out at the river, fixed in ice, bedded under snow. She looked at the brave gay Christmas tree, and thought of the doll beside Mrs. Poppy's bed.

She turned abruptly and gave Mrs. Poppy a big hug and a kiss.

Mrs. Poppy hugged her back. Betsy felt a wet cheek touching her own.

"Betsy!" cried Mrs. Poppy. "Betsy! Why, you've given me a Christmas present!"

And that was the very thing Betsy had wanted to do.

XII

THREE TELEPHONE CALLS

ONE day soon after Mrs. Poppy's party, the telephone at the Ray house rang three times. The last time was the most important of all.

The first time it was for Julia.

She came into the back parlor where Mrs. Ray was sewing and Margaret was playing paper dolls and Betsy was reading *Huckleberry Finn*, a book that Miss Sparrow had picked out for her.

"Mamma," said Julia, looking very pleased. "It's Jerry. The play of *Rip Van Winkle* is coming to town. There's going to be a matinee next Saturday afternoon, and he wants me to go."

"I think that would be lovely," said Mrs. Ray. "That's a wonderful play. Papa and I saw Joseph Jefferson in it, years ago." She seemed as pleased as Julia.

Betsy closed her book, jumped up and went to the back-parlor closet where outdoor wraps were kept.

"Where are you going, Betsy?" asked Mrs. Ray as Julia returned to the telephone.

"To see Winona," said Betsy. "I think she'll want to take Tacy and Tib and me to that matinee." She pulled on her coat with a determined air.

Margaret ran to her mother.

"I wish I could go too, mamma," she said.

"Maybe you can," said Mrs. Ray. "I've half a notion," she added, "to ask papa to take *me*. I've never forgotten that play."

Julia came back from the telephone, and while Betsy strapped on her overshoes and hunted for her mittens, Mrs. Ray told them about Rip Van Winkle. Julia and Betsy knew the story, of course; they had read it in school. But they liked hearing their mother tell about the lovable ne'er-do-well, who played at bowls with a strange ghostly crew in the Kaats-kills, and drank from their flagon, and slept for twenty years.

Mrs. Ray was describing Rip's awakening to find his dog gone, his gun old and rusty and himself with a long white beard, when the telephone rang again. This time it was for Betsy. She returned to the back parlor, dancing.

"It's Winona," she cried. "And she *does* want us to go. Tacy and Tib and me. She has 'comps.'"

"That settles it," said Mrs. Ray to Margaret. "You and I are going too."

As soon as Betsy had finished talking to Winona, Mrs. Ray went to the telephone and gave Central the number of Ray's Shoe Store. Julia and Betsy and Margaret hugged and shouted.

Then Betsy ran out the front door and over to Tacy's. Mrs. Kelly said that Tacy could go; and Betsy and Tacy ran down Hill Street and through the snow-covered vacant lot to Tib's house. Mrs. Muller said that Tib could go; and they all ran on to Winona's.

It had started to snow now, and the whirling, dancing flakes seemed as happy as they were.

Winona had on her wraps when they arrived.

"Let's go look at the billboards," she said.

There were billboards at the end of School Street, a full half-block of them, concealing the slough. The children visited them often, to taste Deep Valley's dramatic fare. Many plays had come to the Opera House since *Uncle Tom's Cabin*, but this was the first matinee.

The bill poster had just finished pasting the large gaudy sheets which announced that the beautiful legendary drama of *Rip Van Winkle* would be shown at the Opera House on Saturday afternoon and evening. They showed pictures of Young Rip, tattered and smiling, with a troop of children at his heels, and Old Rip, waking in the Kaatskills with the white beard Betsy's mother had described; Young Rip with his little daughter, a wee girl wearing a quaint Dutch cap, and that same daughter grown to young womanhood, standing with her sailor lover.

"How can the same actress play first a little girl and then a young lady?" Tib wanted to know.

"A child plays one part, and a woman the other," Winona explained.

"Let's follow that little girl home from the Opera House like we did Little Eva," cried Tacy.

"Let's!" "Let's!"

They were reminded by this of the magic of the other matinee, and they talked about it all the way back to Winona's. It was snowing hard now, and too wet to play out, so they went into Winona's house and played a game of authors.

Tacy and Tib and Winona played; Betsy didn't want to. She asked Winona for a pencil and a piece of paper and sat in a window seat in Winona's father's library. The snow was a spotted veil, concealing trees and houses, but Betsy would not have seen trees and houses anyway. Looking out into the snowstorm, she saw the inside of the Opera House at that dim expectant moment when the curtain went up.

"I've written a poem," she said, returning to the parlor where the game of authors was in progress. "Want to hear it?"

"Sure," said Tacy. She and Tib and Winona were used to listening to what Betsy wrote.

"It's called, *The Curtain Goes Up*," said Betsy.

She read it in a dreamy singsong.

"The lights are turned low,
The violins sing,
A feeling of waiting is
On everything.
Winona and Tib,
And Tacy and me,
We sit very still
In the mystery.
The Opera House feels
Like a big empty cup,
And then something happens,
The curtain goes up.

The curtain goes up,
The curtain goes up,
It's a wonderful moment,
When the curtain goes up.
It's like Christmas morning,
Stealing down stairs,
It's like being frightened,
And saying your prayers,
It's like being hungry
And ready to sup,
It's a wonderful moment,
When the curtain goes up."

"Betsy!" cried Winona. "I like that poem."

Tacy and Tib said that they did too.

"The things you write ought to be published!" Winona declared.

Betsy and Tacy and Tib looked away from one another. The story Tib had printed so neatly on the sheet of pink stationery had never been heard from. As the days went by, they became sadly certain that it never would be heard from.

They were glad now that they had decided not to tell Winona about it.

"Some day they'll be published, maybe," said Betsy in a tone so lacking in her usual soaring confidence that Winona was moved to express unaccustomed praise.

"Some day, nothing!" she exclaimed. "That's as good as the poems in our school reader. I like the part about me. May I have a copy of it, Betsy?"

"You may have the whole thing," said Betsy. "Oh, kids!

Isn't it grand about Saturday? Let's talk about Saturday."

Making a dive for the game of authors, she swept it to the carpet. They began to throw cards.

Winona's mother came in and asked them if they didn't want to make fudge. Perhaps she thought that was a good way to quiet them down. They made fudge, but it was slow hardening, and of course they had to wait for it to harden. Then they had to wait to eat the rich chocolatey squares. It was late when Betsy, Tacy, and Tib started for home.

Just as they left Winona's house they heard the telephone ring.

"That's mamma wanting to know what's become of me," said Betsy.

She did not stop at Tacy's house or Tib's, but hurried through the snowy dark. When she reached home she saw that the dining-room lamp had been lighted. Her father was at home.

She pushed open the kitchen door. The smell of frying ham greeted her first. Right behind that delicious aroma came Margaret.

"Betsy! Betsy!" she cried. "Who do you think telephoned?"

"Wait, Margaret!" Mrs. Ray said. "I want to tell her. Unless you've heard already, Betsy, from Mrs. Muller or Mrs. Kelly?"

"I didn't see them," said Betsy. "What is it?"

"It's something wonderful," cried Julia. She seized Betsy and spun her around the room.

"Me and Margaret, we're going to be in the front row,"

cried Rena. "I wouldn't miss seeing you, Betsy . . ."

"Sh-sh, Rena," said Julia, and Margaret ran to put her hand over Rena's mouth.

"Of course," said Betsy's father, "I have to give my consent." His eyes were twinkling as he stood with his hands in his pockets.

"Mamma! Julia! What is it?" cried Betsy. "Hurry and tell me, please!"

"It's this," said Mrs. Ray. "You and Tacy and Tib and Winona are all going to act in *Rip Van Winkle* Saturday. Both afternoon and evening. Tib will take the part of Mee-

nie, Rip Van Winkle's little girl, and the rest of you are going to be village children."

"What?" cried Betsy. "On the stage?"

"On the stage," her mother answered. "Behind the footlights."

"You'll wear a costume, have grease paint on," babbled Julia.

"I'm taking Margaret," Rena explained.

"Papa and I are coming in the evening," Mrs. Ray added.

Betsy thought she must be dreaming. The kitchen was whirling. The lamp made a yellow track.

"But why? How did it happen?" she asked.

"Sit down, and I'll tell you," her mother said.

Mrs. Poppy, it developed, had telephoned that afternoon. She and Mr. Poppy had received a letter from Minneapolis where the *Rip Van Winkle* company was playing. The manager had said that the little girl who took the part of Meenie, Rip's daughter, had been called back to New York. She was leaving the company when it left the Twin Cities, and the new little Meenie would join them in Omaha.

For the Deep Valley engagement, the manager had asked Mrs. Poppy to find a Deep Valley child. Mrs. Poppy had thought at once of Tib who, although she was twelve years old, was small enough to look much younger.

"She knew Tib could do the part," Mrs. Ray said. "For her dancing has made her accustomed to performing on the stage."

"Oh, Tib will be darling!" cried Betsy. She thought of

Tib with her fluffy yellow curls, wearing a little Dutch cap like the child in the billboard picture. "But how do Tacy and Winona and I happen to be in it?"

"There are village children needed in the play," Mrs. Ray explained, "and it is the custom of the company to get local children for those parts. They haven't any lines to say; they just follow at Rip Van Winkle's heels."

"I know," said Betsy. "I saw us on the billboards."

"Mrs. Poppy thought it might be fun for you to do it."

Betsy felt a wave of love for Mrs. Poppy.

"Tib's part is quite hard," Mrs. Ray went on. "But Mrs. Poppy will teach her. I've talked with the mothers, and all of us think that you children will enjoy the experience."

The kitchen had stopped whirling now. The lamp was fast in its bracket, and its glow was no brighter than the glow on Betsy's face.

Before she ate supper, she telephoned to Winona. That telephone ring they had heard, Winona said, had been Betsy's mother telling the news.

After supper Betsy ran over to Tacy's. Tacy was blissfully scared. In view of the unusual circumstances, she and Betsy were allowed to pay an evening call on Tib.

Tib was calm at the prospect of playing a part on the stage, but she was happy.

"I can do it," she said. "I'll like to do it."

Back at home Betsy sat in front of the hard-coal heater, her arms around her knees. Inside herself she was saying over and over her poem, *The Curtain Goes Up.*

"The curtain goes up,
The curtain goes up,
It's a wonderful moment,
When the curtain goes up . . ."

"When I wrote that poem," she thought, "I didn't know where I'd be when the curtain went up."

She had a vision of the great curtain rising, and herself with Tacy and Tib and Winona, looking out at the dark crowded house from the golden glory of the stage.

XIII

RIP VAN WINKLE

BETSY, Tacy, and Tib made many trips down town that winter but none equaled or even approached in excitement the one they made on Saturday to act in *Rip Van Winkle*.

They walked as far as Winona's house. From there they were driven down in Winona's father's cutter. It had been arranged that Mr. Root would drive them all down. After the matinee each father was to take charge of getting his own child home for supper and back to the Opera House for the evening performance.

Tib had been at the Opera House all morning, rehearsing with the cast. Mrs. Poppy had taught her the part in the several days preceding. New Years had come and gone almost unnoticed, so great was the agitation aroused by Tib's daily visit to the Melborn Hotel.

Tib was not what is called "a quick study"; on the contrary, she was slow. But having learned the part she would not forget it. There was no danger of stage fright or nervousness throwing her off. She would do exactly as she had been told, and Mr. Winter who played the part of Rip had been pleased, Tib said with satisfaction.

"What does he look like?" Winona asked, **as the cutter**

slipped gaily along the polished streets.

"He wears a silk hat, and a diamond ring, and a big gold watch chain. He looks important, and he *is* important, too. I'm supposed to step back and let him cross in front of me. That's one thing I mustn't forget."

"It will seem strange," said Betsy, "to hang on to the coat tails of such an important person."

She and Winona had been told by Mrs. Poppy that they would make their entrance hanging to Rip's coat tails.

"Oh, he's kind," said Tib. "And he likes children. But he's important. Don't forget that."

"Did you try on your costume?" Winona asked.

"Yes. I'm wearing a little Dutch cap like the one we saw in the picture. You all are, I think. And our skirts come down to our ankles. Girls must have dressed that way in Colonial times.

"I ought to look nice," she added. "Mamma washed my hair. And they're going to paint my cheeks."

"We'll all be painted!" Betsy bounced with joy.

"All the kids in our class are coming," said Winona. "Herbert . . . Tom . . ."

"I'm getting scared," said Tacy. Her cheeks didn't need any paint; they were flaming.

"You'll be all right," Betsy assured her. "Just stay close to me."

Mr. Root stopped his horse in front of the Melborn Hotel. They had planned to meet Mrs. Poppy in the lobby there. But she was waiting out in front, walking up and down, more nervous than they had ever seen her.

"I'm as worked up as though I were playing myself," she said when Mr. Root had wished them all luck and driven away.

She put her arm around Tib.

"Girls," she said, "you're going to be proud of Tib today."

"We know it!" shouted Betsy and Tacy. It wasn't the first time they had been proud of Tib.

Winona shouted too. They surrounded Tib like a loyal bodyguard on the walk to the Opera House.

Mrs. Poppy walked bulkily in their midst. She was wearing her sealskin coat and cap; and her yellow hair and the diamonds in her ears gleamed against the fur. She was smiling, but now and then she looked at Betsy with an urgent, almost worried look.

"I'm going to get along all right, Mrs. Poppy," said Betsy. "All of us are."

"Of course you are," said Mrs. Poppy. "It isn't that . . ."

She didn't say what it was.

Sunny Jim darted out of the garage to cheer them on their way. Outside the Opera House a crowd of children had already gathered; they cheered too. All of Deep Valley seemed to know that Betsy, Tacy, Tib, and Winona were acting in *Rip Van Winkle*.

They turned in at the alley that led to the stage door. This was the same door they had seen Little Eva come out of.

"How surprised we'd have been that day," said Betsy, "if we'd known how soon we'd be walking in here ourselves."

"I love to go in doors that say 'Private, Keep Out,'" said Winona.

Tacy said nothing. She hugged her arm through Betsy's as they left their own bright snowy world behind, and entered the theatre.

They found themselves in a dusty barnlike space. They knew it was the stage, because they could see the curtain, half-raised, and the dim empty house beyond. There were stacks of canvas scenery about, and piles of ropes, and an assortment of miscellaneous objects including a wash tub.

"Props," said Tib waving her hand.

Men in overalls were hurrying about.

"Scene shifters," said Tib.

A worried-looking man in a rumpled checked suit approached Mrs. Poppy.

"Mr. Drew, the stage manager," whispered Tib.

Mr. Drew leaned toward Mrs. Poppy. He spoke in a lowered voice, as though he were telling a secret, but his words were audible.

"It's all arranged, Mrs. Poppy," he said. "Mr. . . . er . . . Kee is to show the children their routine. They can dress first."

"Thank you, Mr. Drew," said Mrs. Poppy. "I'm very grateful. This way," she said to the girls and led them down some stairs into a damp-smelling cellar.

They followed a narrow corridor. The walls were covered with show bills. *The Old Homestead. The Silver Slipper. Flora Dora. Ben Hur.* The names, the half-seen brightly colored pictures flashed past in glamorous parade.

Rows of dressing rooms opened off the hall. Tib went into one of them. Betsy, Tacy, and Winona were ushered into another. It contained a cracked mirror, a bare, scratched dressing table, a wash bowl and pitcher, and three wooden chairs.

A small wrinkled old lady with beadlike eyes came in, carrying a bundle of clothing.

"Hello," she said. "I'm Mrs. Mulligan, the wardrobe mistress. These are the costumes for village children, and see that they fit you! I think nothing of snipping off an arm here or a leg there."

Mrs. Mulligan made jokes like that, but she was painstaking about the costumes. Mrs. Poppy came in to help her, and they pinned and fitted energetically.

The dresses were long like Tib's; and the girls wore quaint Dutch caps. Tacy's long red ringlets flowed out becomingly, and so did Winona's straight black locks. Betsy wanted to unbraid her hair, but Mrs. Poppy said "No." She arranged the pigtails so that they stuck out jauntily and tied ribbons on the ends.

Mrs. Poppy painted round red circles on their cheeks. She painted their lips red too. They looked in the mirror at themselves and looked at one another, anticipation bubbling up in laughter.

They ran in to see Tib. She was sitting in front of a mirror. Her yellow hair curled up babyishly around her cap; her cheeks and lips were red like theirs and her lashes were beaded with black.

She wasn't excited in the way the others were, but for Tib she was excited. Her eyes were shining. She looked pleased when they praised her, although she said only:

157

"Thank goodness I'm up in my part!"

She had learned that expression from Mrs. Poppy but she used it naturally. It didn't sound affected coming from Tib as it would have if one of the others had said it.

With Tacy's icy hand in hers and Winona prancing behind, Betsy followed Mrs. Poppy up the stairs. Now the front part of the stage was enclosed; the scenery had been run into place, and the curtain was lowered.

Mr. Drew was waiting in the wings with a tall thin young man who wore a brown wig, knee breeches and a long-tailed coat. Lines were painted on his face.

"Mrs. Poppy," said Mr. Drew. "This is Mr. . . . er . . . Kee. He plays the Vedders, first father, then son."

"And in between," said the young man lightly, "one of Hendrik Hudson's men."

"He understudies Mr. Winter too," said Mr. Drew.

"You sound like an important person," Mrs. Poppy smiled. She put out a white-gloved hand. "How do you do?" she said.

"How do you do?" answered Mr. Kee. He had dancing blue eyes that passed now from Mrs. Poppy to Winona, to Tacy, to Betsy.

"Hello, kids," he said. *Spricht deutsch?*"

"They look as though they should . . . don't they?" Mrs. Poppy asked.

"They're perfect."

"I'd like them to have a very good time."

"So Mr. Drew explained. I'll take care of them," said Mr. Kee. He took Betsy's hand with a flashing smile. "Come

158

on, Braids," he said. "And you, Curls, and Locks. I'll show
you the Village of Falling Water before the curtain goes up."

They went through the wings to the empty stage.

At the back rose the Kaatskill Mountains, brightly purple.
To the left stood a country inn with a swinging sign reading
George III. To the right was a tumble-down cottage.

"Rip Van Winkle's palace," Mr. Kee said. "That's Dame
Van Winkle's wash tub out in front."

"And there's the stool where Tib will be sitting when the
curtain goes up," said Betsy.

"You know the play?"

"Yes. Mrs. Poppy told it to us. We don't know exactly

what we're to do though."

Mr. Kee explained. They came on in the first act, he said. They would wait in the wings until the words: "Here he comes now, surrounded by all the dogs and children in the district. They cling around him like flies around a lump of sugar."

When they got that cue, they would come on stage, running behind Rip.

"Two of us carry his coat tails, Mrs. Poppy says."

"That's right, Braids. Which two shall it be?"

"She and I," said Winona. "Tacy doesn't want to."

"Braids and Locks at the coat tails then, with Curls bringing up the rear." Mr. Kee seemed amused with the names he had made up for them.

He explained further.

"Rip will be carrying a small boy pick-a-back, and another boy will be holding his gun. Those two boys, Tom and Jeff, belong to the company. They know exactly what to do, and you must do just as they do."

"Do we come on and go off when they do?"

"Yes. Stick close to them and you can't go wrong. Don't wander down to the front of the stage or get in anyone's way."

He gave them a few more instructions, then told them that after the first act they would not appear until the fourth.

"You can sit in the wings and watch the play. I'll join you whenever I can. Any questions now?"

"No," said Betsy. "I'm sure we can do it. We give plays ourselves all the time. I'm sure I ought to know how to act," she added importantly. "My uncle is an actor."

"He is?" asked the young man. "What's his name?"

"Keith Warrington." Betsy pronounced it proudly.

"Keith Warrington?"

Mr. Kee sounded so surprised that Betsy asked quickly, "You don't happen to know him; do you?"

"Never heard of him."

The young man settled his wig with long flexible fingers and looked hard at Betsy with his bright blue eyes.

"How do you like that . . . having an uncle in the profession?"

"Oh, I like it," Betsy said.

"She has a trunk full of his costumes," said Winona.

"She uses it for a desk," Tacy put in shyly.

"Desk, eh?" said the young man. "You do your arithmetic there, I suppose?"

"Arithmetic!" said Betsy scornfully. "I write stories there, and poems, and plays."

At that moment two boys in Dutch costume came bounding on the stage.

"Hi, Tom and Jeff!" called the young man. "Come here and meet the 'supes.'" Betsy and Tacy and Winona were "supes," it appeared; that was short for "supernumeraries."

"These are the boys," Mr. Kee explained, "whom you follow through thick and thin."

He walked away.

Tom and Jeff took the girls in hand good-naturedly. They took them to the front of the stage and let them look through a peephole in the center of the curtain. It was bad luck, they explained, to peep from any other place. The girls looked out eagerly and saw the audience filing in, laughing and talking.

"There are Julia and Jerry."

"Katie and Pin are with them."

"I see my father and mother," said Winona.

"I see mine too," said Tacy. "And all the Mullers."

"Rena and Margaret are in the front row," cried Betsy. "Rena's wearing her best hat, with pansies on it."

Winona took another turn at the peephole.

"I can't be sure," she said, "but I *think* I see Tom and Herbert up in the peanut heaven."

There were plenty of boys and girls there to judge by the racket going on.

Through all the noise they could hear the violins being tuned. That thin insistent sound increased the turmoil in their breasts. There was a call for the stage to be cleared, and Tom and Jeff hurried the girls past the Inn of George III, around a canvas wall into the wings. They stood where they could look out on the stage, although they were themselves unseen.

Dame Van Winkle strolled out and took her place at the wash tub. Tib passed by with Mrs. Poppy and sat down on the stool. Mrs. Poppy arranged Tib's cap, the fluffy curls, her skirts. Then Mrs. Poppy rustled off the stage and Tom and Jeff pulled the girls further back in the wings. The orchestra was playing a piece Julia played, Mendelssohn's *Spring Song*.

They could not see the stage now, but they knew what had happened from the hush that fell on everything. Winona leaned out and whispered to Betsy:

"The curtain goes up."

They waited tensely, and after a moment they heard Dame Van Winkle speaking. They heard Tib's voice, sweet and unafraid. They heard Hendrik Vedder, the boy who was little Meenie's friend. Mr. Kee, who was playing Hendrik's father now, would play the grown-up Hendrik later.

Presently Mr. Winter joined the children in the wings. He was dressed in Rip's old deerskin coat, ragged breeches and torn hat, but he did not look merry, as Rip was supposed to look; he looked grave.

He warned the girls in a whisper to stay close to Tom. Unsmiling he hoisted Jeff to his back and handed Tom the

gun. They waited together so silently they could almost hear their heart beats. Tacy reached for Betsy's hand.

They heard a voice. "Here he comes now. . . . They cling around him like flies around a lump of sugar."

Mr. Winter's expression changed; he began to laugh. All at once he was Rip, and Betsy and Winona picked up his coat tails, laughing too. Tacy smiled, although her teeth were chattering. With Jeff riding pick-a-back, they all trooped out into a blaze of light.

After a few minutes Betsy got used to the light. She was conscious of the hushed expectant darkness of the house. Intent only on staying close to Tom and Jeff, she scarcely listened as Rip talked and the Dame scolded, as Meenie and Hendrik and Hendrik's father and themselves went on and off the stage.

Tib did not glance toward her friends. She too was intent . . . upon saying her lines and doing exactly as she had been told. But in the dance that ended the act, she gave them a cloudless smile.

When the curtain went up after having gone down, and the principals went forward to receive their applause, Tib floated out. She held Rip's hand with one hand and with the other she lifted her skirt in the daintiest of curtseys. Beyond the footlights her family and friends and half of Deep Valley, it seemed, clapped and cheered approval of the play, and especially of Tib. Modest but pleased, she curtsied again and again. The curtain went down.

Betsy, Tacy, Tib, and Winona did not appear in the second act. Mr. Kee placed chairs for them in the wings at a point where they could see the stage, and while they waited for the curtain to go up, he dropped casually down on a barrel.

He stretched his long arms and locked his hands behind his head.

"Tell me," he said to Betsy, "why you use a trunk for a desk."

"It's much nicer than an ordinary desk," said Betsy. "A real theatrical trunk!"

"How do you happen to have it at your house?"

Betsy, talkative as always, explained.

She told him how Uncle Keith had run away from home, and why; she told how his trunk had come back at the outset of the Spanish War, and had never been called for, and how no one knew where he was.

"But he'll come back some day," Betsy said. "He must want to see mamma, just as she wants to see him."

"*Does* she want to see him?" asked the young man. But just then the bell rang as a warning that the act was about to begin. Without waiting for an answer, he jumped up and strode away.

"It's a good idea, Betsy," said Tacy, "to tell that actor about your Uncle Keith. Maybe he'll meet him some day."

"He seems so interested too," said Betsy.

"Hush now!" cried Winona. "There's the music."

The curtain rose slowly on the dimly lighted kitchen of Rip's house.

Meenie sat by the window, looking out at a raging storm. It would be interesting, Betsy thought, to run around in back

and see how they made that storm . . . the rain, the fright-
ful wind, the thunder, and the lightning flashes. But she
could not bear to take her eyes from Tib.

As the act progressed, however, she forgot that Meenie
was Tib. Lost in the drama, she looked and listened, while
the boy Hendrik told Meenie tales of the spirits that played
at nine pins in the mountains, while Rip and his wife quarreled and Dame Van Winkle turned the hapless fellow out
into the torrent. She forgot it was Tib's treble saying:

"Oh mother, hark at the storm!"

Again Tib curtsied before the big curtain, holding Rip's
hand.

Between the second and third acts, Mr. Kee came to talk
with the girls again. He was dressed as one of Hendrik Hudson's ghostly crew, wearing a high-crowned hat and gray
doublet and hose.

He dropped down on his barrel.

"I suppose," he said to Betsy, "your family is all here to
see you act."

"Papa and mamma are coming tonight," said Betsy. "But
Rena and Margaret and Jerry and Julia are here."

"How many brothers and sisters do you have?" he exclaimed, sounding surprised.

"Only two," said Betsy. "Jerry is a friend of Julia's. He
invited her to come and see the play. And Rena is our hired
girl. She brought Margaret."

"Is Julia old enough to be coming to a play with a young
man?" Mr. Kee seemed amazed.

"Of course," said Betsy. "Why shouldn't she be?"

"She's in high school," said Tacy.

"You ought to hear her sing, Mr. Kee," Winona said. "She sings and speaks pieces too."

Betsy explained.

"She takes after Uncle Keith."

"She . . . what?" The young man jumped up as though he had heard the bell. But he hadn't. Erect on his long legs, he stood still, staring at Betsy.

"Does she look like him?" he asked abruptly.

"No," said Betsy. "Julia and Margaret and I all have dark hair like our father's. Uncle Keith has red hair like our mother's. But Julia gets her talent for singing and acting from Uncle Keith, and I get my writing from him."

"You do?"

"That's what my mother says," answered Betsy firmly. "And my father says so too."

The bell really did ring then, and in a few moments they were transported to a wild mountain glen. Rip played at nine pins with an eerie crew; he drank from their flagon.

As soon as the act ended, Mr. Kee appeared.

"Braids," he said. "Let's take a look through the curtain. If I were ever to meet this uncle of yours, I'd like to be able to tell him I'd seen his family."

"Mr. Kee," said Betsy. "That's a splendid idea."

They went to the peephole in the curtain.

Margaret was acting very ladylike. Every hair of the brown English bob was in place. She was turning her big eyes solemnly about.

Julia was chatting with Jerry, looking very grown-up, with

167

a fluffy bow at the top of her pompadour and another at the back of her neck.

"Father and mother coming tonight, eh?" asked Mr. Kee.

"Yes," said Betsy. "Papa can't get away from the store in the afternoon."

"What about your grandparents?" Mr. Kee asked. "The peppery old gentleman you told me about? I don't suppose *he*'d come to see a play."

"He and Grandma live in California now," Betsy replied. "He isn't as peppery as he used to be. Mamma thinks he's sorry he made Uncle Keith run away."

"He didn't actually *make* him run away," said the young man.

"Oh, yes he did!" answered Betsy.

"Not in my opinion," said Mr. Kee. "The young man must have been plenty peppery himself. You told me he had red hair, you know. He certainly gave everyone plenty of worry, and now, probably, he's ashamed to come back."

"*Ashamed* to come *back?*" Betsy cried. The honest surprise in her voice made Mr. Kee start.

"Why, that's the silliest thing I ever heard in my life!" she cried. "Everyone is longing for him to come back. It would make my mother happier than anything else in the world. He ought to be ashamed of *not* coming back."

"Hmm! You think so? Hmm!" said Mr. Kee.

The last act was in several scenes. Rip woke from his twenty-year nap. Wrinkled and ancient, with his flowing white beard, he returned to the village to find George III replaced by George Washington on the Inn's swinging sign.

Betsy, Tacy, and Winona were part of a crowd hooting cruelly at the old man's heels.

No one believed the story of his long sleep in the Kaatskills. His old friends were dead, his wife was married to someone else, and Meenie (now a young lady, and played by a young lady actress) was about to be forced into marriage with a villain.

Mr. Kee appeared in the very nick of time, as the dashing sailor, Hendrik Vedder, come home to claim his sweetheart. Rip was recognized; he got his wife back; he came into a fortune, and he gave Meenie to Hendrik.

Everything came out right, before Rip raised his glass.

"Here's to your good health, und to your family's, und may you all live long and prosper!"

No wonder the audience almost wore out its hands with clapping!

Again and again the company appeared before the curtain. Betsy, Tacy, and Winona went now, trying to curtsey like Tib, smiling broadly at their respective families. Their classmates in the peanut gallery shouted and whooped. It was glorious! Like all glorious things it had to end, but unlike most of them it was going to be repeated that night, right after supper.

The girls scampered down to the basement to get into their own clothes. They washed their faces but were careful to leave some actress-red on their cheeks. They rushed back up to the stage door where their families were gathered. Betsy saw Jerry and Julia, Rena and Margaret. Her father, she knew, would be out in the alley, holding Old Mag.

To her surprise and pleasure she recognized Mr. Kee in the crowd around the door. In street clothes, he was tall and slender with a sweep of dramatic red hair.

"Braids," he said to Betsy, coming forward, "what do you think your mother is having for supper?"

Betsy was surprised at the question.

"Why . . . fried potatoes, probably," she said.

"Just what I thought," the young man answered. "In that case, I'm going home with you."

"You're . . . coming . . . home with me?" Betsy was delighted and bewildered.

"The reason I'm coming home with you," Mr. Kee said confidentially, "is that your mother fries potatoes so extremely well."

He smiled at her, his bright eyes dancing. He had a smile like . . . like . . . like . . .

"Uncle Keith!" cried Betsy. She tumbled into his arms.

Echoes to her cry sprang up all around her.

"Uncle Keith!" cried Tacy.

"Uncle Keith!" cried Tib.

"Uncle Keith!" cried Winona, and Julia, and Margaret, and even Rena.

Mr. Ray, out in the alley, heard the cries; he left Old Mag standing alone and pushed his way in at the door and found the young man's hand.

Dancing about in delirious joy, Betsy saw Mrs. Poppy. She was standing a little distance away, watching them and smiling. Her eyes looked as though she were ready to cry.

XIV

THE CURTAIN GOES UP

THE sleigh was crowded going home, but nobody minded. In the back seat Margaret sat on Rena's lap, and Julia and Betsy sat close together squeezing each other's hands. They did not talk much. The great adventure of the play was dimmed by the far greater adventure of finding Uncle Keith.

In the front seat Uncle Keith talked in a quick earnest voice. He sat with his arm along the back of the seat, his face turned to Mr. Ray's kindly and now serious face. Uncle Keith wore a fur coat and a broad-brimmed actorish hat. His deep voice ran on and on beneath the chime of sleigh bells and the beat of Old Mag's hoofs.

He seemed to be pouring out the story of his wanderings. He *had* been in the Spanish War, the girls heard him say. He had been at Santiago. As an actor he had not done too badly; he had had his ups and downs; all actors had. The present engagement was with a solid company. But it had not satisfied his pride; he had not been willing to make his presence known in his own home town . . . until he met Betsy.

He turned with his flashing smile.

Mr. Ray turned, too.

"We must plan quickly how we're going to surprise mother."

There was a clamor of voices then, for everyone had an idea. Mr. Ray wanted Uncle Keith to rap at the kitchen door and pretend he was delivering groceries. Margaret thought he should go down the chimney like Santa Claus. Julia wanted him to stand underneath the window and sing a serenade.

Rena thought Mrs. Ray should be prepared.

"She might have an attack," said Rena. "Lord-a-mercy, it's the last thing in her mind to have her long-lost brother walking in."

"But she's never had an attack," said Mr. Ray. "She doesn't have attacks. What's your idea, Betsy?"

Betsy bounced beneath the buffalo robe.

"Let's take a scene out of the play," she cried. "You be Rip, Uncle Keith, and take Margaret on your back, and Julia and I will carry your coat tails, and all of us will prance through the kitchen door."

"Betsy has picked it," said Uncle Keith. "That's just what we will do."

They climbed out of the sleigh on the little road that led around to the barn.

"I'll be along to give you some supper," Mr. Ray told Old

Mag, slapping her bay rump.

Old Mag went on without a driver. The conspirators tiptoed over the snowy lawn and looked in at the kitchen window.

Sure enough, Mrs. Ray was frying potatoes. She was dressed for the theatre, in her green broadcloth dress . . . it was that shade of soft green which was most becoming to her. She wore a green bow in her high red pompadour. A fresh checkered apron was tied around her waist.

"Still as slim as a breeze," said Uncle Keith.

"She's a wonder," said Mr. Ray.

He pushed open the side kitchen door.

"Hi, Jule! Want to see a scene from the play?"

"Is my actress daughter in it?" Mrs. Ray asked, laughing.

"There are plenty of actors in it," said Mr. Ray.

"Well, hurry up with it. You're letting the cold in."

But he held the door open a minute.

Uncle Keith put his hat on the back of his head and shook his red hair into his eyes. He picked up Margaret and swung her to his back. Julia and Betsy took hold of his coat tails.

"We laugh and yell," Betsy explained.

Laughing and yelling, they all trooped into the kitchen.

The long-handled fork Mrs. Ray was holding clattered to the floor. She turned so pale that it looked for a moment as though Rena might have been right about that attack. But instantly a wave of color rushed back into her cheeks. Joyful tears filled her eyes, and she ran to Uncle Keith who flung his arms about her.

Julia and Betsy and Margaret stood silent and abashed.

Rena wiped her eyes, saying "Lord-a-mercy!" "Lord-a-mercy!" over and over again. Mr. Ray's eyes looked dampish too.

"Now, now! There, there!" he kept saying, for Betsy's mother was crying hard. Uncle Keith was crying too, and presently Julia began to sniff, and then Betsy did, and then Margaret.

"Make some coffee, Rena," Mr. Ray said. "Come on, you idiots, and cry in the parlor, so that Rena can get supper on. I'm going out to feed Old Mag. She's got more sense than you have."

That made them all laugh, and Rena took off her coat and her best hat with pansies on it, and tied on an apron. When Mr. Ray came back from the barn the family was in the back parlor. The crying was over, and everyone was talking at once trying to explain to Mrs. Ray just what had happened.

"I didn't know he was Uncle Keith because his name was Mr. Kee," Betsy said.

"Mr. Kee?" Mrs. Ray asked.

"Yes," said Uncle Keith. "I act under two names usually, Waring Kee for the Nicholas Vedder part, and Keith Warrington for Hendrik. But I asked to be programmed only as Waring Kee in Deep Valley."

"Why did you do that, Keith?" Mrs. Ray asked, holding his hands. "Would you really have come to Deep Valley and gone away without seeing me?"

"I'm afraid I would have," said Uncle Keith, looking ashamed, "if Braids here hadn't told me you'd forgiven me."

"Then how lucky, how incredibly lucky, that you and Betsy happened to get acquainted!"

Uncle Keith smoothed back his red hair thoughtfully.

"That wasn't just luck," he said. "Somebody managed it. I felt there was something funny in the air when Drew, the stage manager, asked me to look after the 'supes.' That's never part of my job. He said it was a favor the theatre owner's wife had asked . . ."

"Mrs. Poppy," said Betsy. "I heard her thank Mr. Drew for arranging it."

"Mrs. Poppy!" exclaimed Mrs. Ray. "But how could she have known who he was?"

"I told her about Uncle Keith long ago," said Betsy. "She's been making inquiries about him. She asked me not to tell you, mamma, because she didn't want you disappointed in case she didn't find him."

"She saw the name Kee Waring, no doubt, and thought that was an easy change from Keith Warrington," Mr. Ray said.

"Or she may have looked up a Minneapolis program. I was Keith Warrington there," said Uncle Keith.

As it came out later, both these things had happened. Mrs. Poppy had seen the name Kee Waring, and thinking it sounded like Keith Warrington had asked Mr. Poppy to get a Minneapolis program. She had received one just a few minutes before Betsy, Tacy, Tib, and Winona had found her pacing back and forth in front of the hotel.

Mrs. Ray's eyes grew soft as Mrs. Poppy's part in the affair became clear.

"How very very kind of her!" she said. "From now on, Betsy, Mrs. Poppy is my friend as well as yours."

"Will you call on her?" asked Betsy.

"With my card case and Old Mag, just as you asked me to," Mrs. Ray answered, smiling.

"Will you take me?" asked Julia. "Remember what Betsy said about her helping me with my singing."

"I'll take you too," Mrs. Ray promised.

Betsy knew then that Mrs. Poppy's wish was coming true.

All talking at once, they moved to the dining room, where Uncle Keith ate fried potatoes with one arm around Mrs. Ray and Margaret on his lap. He kept looking across the table at Julia and Betsy with his dancing bright blue eyes.

Rena had made a pot of coffee, good and strong. And she had stirred up some biscuits to go with the fried potatoes and cold meat. Without being told, she had opened some Damson plum preserves. It was a good supper, but only the children ate much.

Uncle Keith kept looking around the table at the faces under the hanging lamp as though he couldn't look at them enough.

After supper Betsy took him upstairs to see her desk.

"I suppose you'll want your trunk now," she said. "And that's all right. I can get another desk."

"Don't you dare!" he said. "Braids, some of the stories and poems I've always wanted to write are going to be written on this trunk."

Betsy liked to hear him say that. It made her feel better about the sheet of pink stationery that had gone to the

Ladies' Home Journal and had never been heard from.

When they got down stairs, Uncle Keith asked Julia to sing for him. She sang a new song called *The Rosary*, and she sang it so well that Uncle Keith got up and kissed her.

Mr. Ray went out to the front porch and brought in the newspaper.

"Thought I'd see what the *Sun* had to say about your show," he remarked, unfolding it.

"Good gosh!" said Uncle Keith to Betsy, jumping up. "You and I have to get back to the theatre."

He looked around for his coat and hat, and Julia ran to get them for him. Betsy started putting on her wraps too.

"Can you come back here to stay tonight?" Betsy's mother asked.

"Yes, I can. Tomorrow's Sunday. I can take the train to Omaha tomorrow night."

"I'll bring Old Mag around right away," Mr. Ray said.

He delayed, though, to glance at the newspaper. And then he did not move.

"The notice of the play will be on the inside, dear," Mrs. Ray said, but Mr. Ray did not open the paper further. He stared at the front page.

"Well, bless my soul!" he said at last, in such an unbelieving tone that everyone started. Julia ran to look over his shoulder.

"Betsy!" she cried.

Dropping her overshoes, Betsy ran to look. She could hardly believe her eyes at what she saw.

There on the front page of Winona's father's paper, in

the very center of the page, enclosed in a decorative box made of roses and doves, was a poem. The title was printed at the top and the author's name at the bottom.

The title was, *The Curtain Goes Up.*

The author's name was Betsy Warrington Ray.

"Why, Betsy, how did this happen?" her mother asked in an agitated voice.

"I don't know," said Betsy. "I've no idea."

"Did you send the poem to the paper?"

"No. But I gave it to Winona. She asked me for it. She liked it."

"Liked it!" said Mrs. Ray. "I should think she *would* like it. It's splendid! It's wonderful."

Mrs. Ray always thought that about her children's achievements.

"I love it!" cried Julia.

"Couldn't have done better myself," said Mr. Ray.

Rena came running from the kitchen to look, and Margaret took the paper into her chubby hands.

Uncle Keith was all ready to leave for the theatre. He had put on his fur coat, and his hat was in his hand. He was in a hurry, but he didn't act hurried.

Standing in the middle of the Ray front parlor, he read Betsy's poem aloud.

Betsy's father stood listening, trying not to look proud. Betsy's mother was crying for the second time that night. Margaret's face was shining as though it had been buttered. And Julia held Betsy's hand tight.

Uncle Keith read the poem aloud in his beautiful trained

actor's voice. It wasn't as good as he made it sound; Betsy knew that. But it was good enough so that she felt as she listened that some day she could write something good. Some day in her maple or on Uncle Keith's trunk, she would write something good.

Tacy would be proud, and so would Tib. And so would Winona who had brought about the present golden moment. And so would Miss Sparrow who had helped her at the library. And so would dear Mrs. Poppy on whom her mother would call.

Thoughts are such fleet magic things. Betsy's thoughts swept a wide arc while Uncle Keith read her poem aloud. She thought of Julia learning to sing with Mrs. Poppy. She thought of Tib learning to dance. She thought of herself and Tacy and Tib going into their 'teens. She even thought of Tom and Herbert and of how, by and by, they would be carrying her books and Tacy's and Tib's up the hill from high school.

> "The curtain goes up,
> The curtain goes up . . ."

Uncle Keith read in his vibrant actor's voice.

THE END

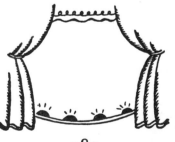